Just as I rea⬛⬛⬛ ⬛⬛⬛⬛⬛⬛ ⬛⬛⬛ ⬛⬛⬛d the
front door op⬛

Was that a sud⬛⬛⬛ ⬛⬛⬛⬛⬛⬛⬛ ⬛⬛⬛ ⬛⬛⬛⬛⬛ Had
I left it ajar? I c⬛⬛⬛⬛ ⬛⬛⬛⬛ make myself breathe. Then I
heard a sound that hammered the final nail into my
coffin of terror. The front door moaned shut. And not
like the wind sucking it back, but a deliberate closure
followed by a shuffling of feet.

   Wind does not shuffle.

   My body went into high alert. I leaned down to see
a man standing in the entry. No waiting for a buildup
of nerves. Fear injected itself straight into my veins.

Another Stab at Life

Anita Higman

HEARTSONG
PRESENTS
MYSTERIES

Dedication
To my husband, Peter. Happy silver anniversary. And thanks for your
encouragement all these years. Your faithful support has made all the
difference.

Acknowledgments
A warm hug goes to my aunt Reny "Beanie" Powers. You taught me that laughter
and joy are presents from God, and that we should most certainly open them.
What a blessing to watch you live the scripture, "A cheerful heart is good
medicine" (Proverbs 17:22 NIV).

Gratitude also goes to Barbour editors Susan Downs and Lynda Sampson for
their insightful editorial assistance, to author DiAnn Mills for her generous help,
and to my daughter, Hillary, for her creative input.

Psalm 121:8
The LORD will watch over your coming and going
both now and forevermore.

A Book Lover's Hope

One wishes for lights in upper windows,
for shadows, a gasp, and voices that travel.
Oh, for romance and love, a twist of fate,
and a gothic mystery to unravel.
Anita Higman

ISBN 978-1-59789-516-3

Cover Design: Kirk DouPonce, DogEared Design
Cover Illustration: Jody Williams

*Our mission is to publish and distribute inspirational products offering exceptional
value and biblical encouragement to the masses.*

Printed in the U.S.A.

Irony at Its Best

What a steamy night for breathing. The August air dripped with a tropical heat that could make sweating an amateur sport. It's one reason I vowed never to call Houston home.

I glanced in the rearview mirror at my dissolving makeup and wooly hair. "Wow. Serious meltdown."

I groaned one of those long and inward groans that only God could hear. *How did this happen? Here I am, driving to my newly inherited home, a sinister-looking mansion nestled in the heart of. . .Houston.*

"Irony at its best," I whispered. "Bailey Marie Walker, you will not have a nervous breakdown," I muttered to myself. "There's no time for it, and there's certainly no money."

I assessed my surroundings. Towering pines jutted up on both sides. The darkening sky sealed off the tomblike passage. Storm clouds. I hoped they didn't decide to stay and play.

Suddenly my car's right front tire plunged into a hole. I yanked the wheel to the right, sending my vehicle careening toward a tree. I swung back just in time to avert a disaster. With a clawlike grip on the wheel and ragged breathing, I steered my car ever so slowly back onto the road. I wondered if the pothole was allegorical somehow.

I felt like pounding something, but I knew it would be wasted energy. *Okay. God, maybe I need some help here. I've lost everything. My family. My job. My apartment. Our friend Job is starting to look like a long-lost relative. Lord, I'm really not talking to myself here, am I?* I felt my forehead, noticing my recently sprouted frown lines.

I turned the corner onto my new street, Midnight Falls. *Is that supposed to be a joke?* I cut the engine to take in a deep visual drink of the surroundings. In general, the neighborhood didn't look too dire, since some of the other houses appeared refurbished, but a little gasp escaped my mouth as my gaze landed on my ghoulish-looking mansion. The house, which was illuminated only by the full moon and the street lamps, rose up like a medieval horror with its two stories of wood and stone, a third-story belfry-looking tower with a spire, and Gothic windows. But hopefully, no dungeon.

The house had been an indulgence when Granny was young. She'd purchased the home not to live in, but because it looked exactly like a house from one of her nightmares. Granny had been madcap in her approach to life, but this house was certainly more macabre than madcap.

"Wow. And I'm going to make my home in that thing?" I mumbled. I think my frown lines deepened just then. Out of desperation, I decided to think of a positive. The house did appear very spacious, and it certainly had a lot of personality, but besides the creep factor, its chipped gray paint, moldering stone, and drooping balustrades stole away any possible bragging rights. Portions of the house were even covered with vines as if it were hiding like a guilty child.

Bottom line—no putting a pretty face on this ugly reality—the house was one gargantuan wreck. In fact, if I did an appraisal tonight, I'd probably be in the hole because somebody would want to charge me to tear it down.

Shame pinched at my heart. *I'm not acting grateful for this love-gift from Granny Minna, am I, God?*

Still, too bad Granny's attorney, Mr. Lakes, hadn't given me more information. He'd just licked his slightly bluish lips and said, "You might discover a certain. . . unwholesomeness about the house. . .which you may find on occasion. . .disconcerting." Then Mr. Lakes took a long puff on his cigar as he tossed me the key. And that was that. Before I could inquire as to what horror awaited me, I was jostled out the door with a deed, a key, and copious amounts of anxiety, all offered by a lawyer who sported a fake British accent and an unmatched plaid suit. I hadn't known which to be more terrified of—the house or the malodorous Mr. Lakes.

I drove up to the house and got out of my car. *Come on. I'm a survivor. Not a wimp.* I rolled the corroded key around in my fingers as I glared up at the house. *This is a* really *old building, but I can make it a home. Somehow. Eventually.* But why was there always a prologue to every story in my life? *And why can't I get my hands to stop shaking?*

I looked from the house to my meager possessions in my pretend luxury car with no air conditioning. How could a Realtor get into such a mess? We're not the kind to feed off angst. I sighed, grabbed some of my belongings, and started up the walk.

The key in my hand suddenly glowed. I stared upward. The full moon, which had broken free from the storm clouds, bathed the neighborhood in an unearthly radiance. How fitting. I wondered if one could get a werewolf howl as a freebie along with the lunar show.

The house also brightened in the moon's light, but it looked older and peelier than ever, with a sufficient number of bare windows to keep the local peeping toms in business for years. Even the square tower with the spire had casements. Or was that a turret instead of a tower? Guess if I'd learned my architectural terminology better while I was training in Oklahoma City, I would have made more money as a Realtor. And if I'd made more money as a Realtor, maybe they wouldn't have let me go.

I yanked the iron gate open a little harder than I needed to. The pathetic thing wobbled off its rusty hinges and fell with a loud clanking sound on the sidewalk.

Smart move, Bailey. I glanced around. All quiet again. "Whew."

With cautious steps, I headed up the path to the front door. Some creature, which gave off a quack like a duck, ceased its performance. Now all my own noises seemed amplified. My shoes crunched on the cement walkway as if they were attached to microphones. Like the weighty cadence of an Edgar Allan Poe poem, each grinding step made its own lonely statement.

Oh brother. My imagination had definitely kicked in. *Come on, Bailey. Just a few more steps.*

As I walked toward the house, I quietly sang whatever popped into my head. I tried "A Mighty Fortress Is Our God" to a jazzier rhythm. Even when I was a kid, singing had always helped me melt away all things frightening.

I caught a whiff of roses. Nice. But brambly weeds tore at my legs. I swiped away a vine caught on my capris and then climbed up the steps to the front door. I peered in the bare windows hoping a Cyclops wouldn't appear. No faces materialized, one-eyed or otherwise. No one at all. In fact, except for the attorney who'd given me the key, no one on earth knew I'd come.

I steadied my right hand to get the key into the hole. "I have nowhere else to go, so this is it," I said, giving myself a pep talk. My finances were in such disarray, I couldn't even afford a hotel. "Open this door, Bailey!" I yelled. "Now." Then I shushed myself so the neighbors wouldn't release a pack of mongrels on me.

I expelled some air I'd been holding in. Fortunately, there was substantial space between the houses, and each home was made more private by enormous cedar trees. But in spite of the seclusion, I noticed something coming from the neighbor's house—a strange blinking light, which appeared to come from the upper window. Not just a flashing light, but what appeared to be Morse code. *Whatever happened to cell phones?*

I stopped for a second to see if I could make out the signal. I'd learned a bit of the code from a mystery I once read entitled *Laid Out in Lavender.*

Okay, there's a dot and dash. And then a dash. A and T. The word "at." What does that mean? I must have missed the first letter. Okay, this is ridiculous, Bailey. It's just some kid messing around with a flashlight.

I turned my attention to the business at hand, and bit by bit, I turned the key. Success. I smashed the lever down and pushed the huge ornate door. Nothing. No movement. *Okay, looks like you're going to put up a fight.* "You want trouble?" I asked as I gave the heavy door another prizefighter shove with my left arm. Either the key didn't work, or the door had swelled shut just like the rest of my life. Probably swollen with the same humidity that made my wiry hair look like Medusa.

Maybe I could sleep out on the damp, insect-infested

lawn tonight. With that thought, I gave the door one more heave with my shoulder. The door flew open in a wild swing, causing me to burst into the house.

After I recovered, I dragged my stuff inside and flicked on my jumbo flashlight. I shined the beam around, stepping gingerly about, half expecting the floors to give way into another dimension.

I shined the beam upward and took in a rather formidable-looking entryway with a vaulted ceiling. The heat and moldy odors nearly snatched my breath away. Such an oppressive, airless place, as if the rooms were waiting to inhale.

Bailey, get a grip.

The words of Mr. Lakes could almost be heard in the still room: "There's an unwholesomeness about the house, which you may find disconcerting." *I should have come in the daylight. What was I thinking?*

As I maneuvered my light around, I saw a large dining hall to my right and, to my left, an even larger living area, which was embellished with a gray stone fireplace. On both sides of the hearth, carved figures were positioned as though they were holding up the mantle. I moved in closer.

Gargoyles, no less. Oh, my. If I hadn't been so shaky I would have laughed. "Granny, you had the most remarkable sense of humor of anyone I've ever known." The sound of my voice echoed slightly through the living room, making me shudder.

I backed up slowly and then bumped into an old couch. Rather than sitting, I took in a deep breath for support. *Okay. What next?* I swiveled my beam between the two main rooms and discovered a rather decrepit-looking staircase curving its way up to the second story. Just left of the staircase was a hallway crowned with a pointed archway. I stood there for a moment, taking in the whole of what I'd seen so far. The house must have been grand when it was built ages ago, but now it was definitely a timeworn relic. "It probably has hieroglyphics for wallpaper." I chuckled nervously at my own joke.

I suddenly noticed a switch on the wall. *Well, someone must have modernized a bit.* But surely the lights didn't work. I flipped the switch up. Lights! I couldn't believe it. That was *way* too easy. Even though the lights were bare bulbs, a bit of my confidence returned. The house certainly gave me the creepy crawlies—kind of like a tarantula tiptoeing on my bed pillow—but I knew the worst was over. Light had come into my shadowy world. But who had turned on the electricity? Certainly not the illustrious Mr. Lakes.

Taking advantage of the illumination, I glanced around again. *Boy, this house certainly wouldn't show well to a buyer.* My gaze fell, and I noticed something by the staircase. A big box with a pretty bow sat there as if just waiting to be opened. *A present for me?* Couldn't be a housewarming gift from Lakes, yet he was the only one who knew I was coming. *Oh, well. Maybe there's a glimmer of humanity in him.*

As I tugged at the orange bow, I realized the container was taped shut. Heavily taped shut. I picked up the box and gave it a shake or two, but the weight seemed unbalanced as the insides shifted awkwardly. *Well, whoever sent it, I hope they have expensive taste.* I set the box back down, and with one grappling movement, I raked my finger across the tape. My stomach growled, and I suddenly hoped the contents of the box included something to eat.

I lifted the lid and took a peek inside. I stumbled backward, shattering the air with screams. A cat lay lifeless in the box, its green eyes still open. My hands slapped against the floor, trying to catch myself, but I landed hard. I scooted myself away from the box until I backed against the front wall. I hugged my arms around my knees, hoping for comfort.

One short phrase echoed in my head. Who would do such a thing to a helpless cat? Was it Lakes? How could it be? He was an insensitive moron with a weird gleam in his eye, but Granny must have found something redeeming in him, especially since she'd kept him as her attorney even after she'd moved from Oklahoma. And surely Lakes had better things to do than drive all that way just to give me a dead cat.

Was someone trying to scare me? But why? Who would want this place? *I don't even know if I want this place. It's a mess. It's one huge, gargantuan mess! And my housewarming gift is a dead animal!* I screamed again for good measure. I felt a little better.

From across the room, I glared at the package, which was really a tiny casket. The box seemed to stare back, mocking me.

Okay, the situation did indeed fall into the category of ghastly, but I could get through ghastly. I had before. Maybe another scream would be helpful. I paused, ready to let another one fly, but decided to groan instead. My throat already hurt from screeching. I was grateful I hadn't eaten much all day, since a dry heave seemed to be working its way up my stomach. I coughed and swallowed hard.

A plan. I needed a plan.

Okay, I'm going to get up and mosey over to the box. Then I'm going to place it outside and bury the poor thing in the morning. I sat still. Apparently, I hadn't heard my own orders.

I shivered. *God help me. What do I do?*

I finally rose and strolled over to the box. As I peered over the edge of the package and gazed at the cat again, I couldn't believe how alive it looked. The animal had no injuries, yet I knew the thing was dead by the way its neck was resting at an odd angle.

Even though my mind was reeling, I forced myself to focus. If the cat had been dead for days, the stench would have been stifling. Yet there was no odor. I moved in for a closer inspection. The sides were lined with plastic, and claw marks were visible all around the inside of the container. Whoever did this deed was a monster. The cat had obviously been put in the box alive, and then it gradually suffocated.

Bailey, stay calm. I could place the cat outside on the front porch tonight and then bury the poor thing in the morning.

I suddenly thought of the more menacing ramifications of my grisly present. If no one had the key but me, then how did someone get in my house? That's breaking and entering and the little gift was called *harassment*.

But most important, was the perpetrator just trying to play a demented trick on me, or did the culprit have darker intentions? Oh, I was going to lose a lot of sleep over that one. I knew what my Realtor coworkers would say back in Oklahoma. They'd say, "Why don't you just call the police?" But ever since my police officer fiancé, Sam, turned to the dark side, I hadn't been one just to ring up my local sheriff. Especially since he'd hired somebody to wreck my apartment just to remind me he was trashing our relationship so he could marry my best friend. Yeah, boy, it was hard to forget that little piece of history.

So, I would handle this incident on my own, even if I had to buy a gun to protect myself. Although I'd probably end up shooting my toe off or worse. But even with the fear growing inside me, there was a kernel of something else—a resolve not to allow anyone to manipulate or terrorize me.

I sighed as I looked at the box again. In a sudden rush of adrenaline-laced courage, I closed the box tightly and hid it on my front porch.

Before I collapsed from exhaustion, I'd need to search each room to make certain no one was prowling around, and then I'd have to find a bed. I felt so wiped out I wouldn't even be able to fend off any monsters should any decide to have me for a midnight snack.

I stopped in front of a moldy mirror in the hallway; one that looked like it had been feeding on itself for sustenance. I leaned in for a closer look. Besides the lingering terror in my eyes, I simply appeared tired. But oddly, my crow's-feet seemed softer, my face rosier. *How did that happen?* My gray eyes hadn't become dazzling, but my frizzy shoulder-length auburn hair had turned into damp ringlets. Maybe humidity had its upside. "Kind of schoolgirlish, but not bad," I said to the mirror, hoping to lighten my anxieties. *But enough cosmetology updates.*

Time to snoop through the rest of the downstairs. First, the hall closet. Deep and dark, but no scary visitors there. Or dead cats. Emptiness never looked so good.

Then I found the downstairs bathroom. Needing to freshen, I turned on the faucet. Rusty liquid spewed and then something like real water gushed out. I splashed my face and rinsed my hands. *Ahhh.* That cool water felt good. Of course, there were no towels, so I dried myself off on my shirt. Okay, bathroom, weird, but doable with decontamination. Mental note—buy disinfectant.

Next, a cavelike hallway led to an extended kitchen with an adjoining sitting room. Wow. Ancient, but roomy. I flipped on more lights and noticed some chairs that looked as if they'd been excavated from the city dump. Out of curiosity, I pounded my fist on one of the chairs. Dust rose up in a suffocating brown cloud, making me sneeze. *Okay, moving on.* Another hallway led to the east side of the house. Leaded glass doors opened into a smoking-jacket-type library, but thankfully, the only things dwelling there were shelves upon shelves of dusty books. Secure? Check.

After exploring the first floor, I slowly made my way up the stairs. I listened to the creaking of every single step, concerned that the whole staircase would collapse. Finally, after a few more steps, I realized the wood was solid. *Perhaps it's only the railing that's crumbling.* But as I tiptoed closer to the first landing, just before the stairs made their turn, the murkiness and the groaning steps began to take their toll. Suddenly scenes from every scary movie I'd ever seen started to flash before me.

"If you silly stairs didn't creak, I would be disappointed," I told them.

I started up another hymn and could almost hear Granny's words. "You can do anything, Bailey girl."

My shoulders relaxed a bit.

Just as I reached for a light switch, I heard the front door open. Was that a sudden breeze playing with the door? Had I left it ajar? I couldn't make myself breathe. Then I heard a sound that hammered the final nail into my coffin of terror. The front door moaned shut. And not like the wind sucking it back, but a deliberate closure followed by a shuffling of feet.

Wind does not shuffle.

My body went into high alert. I leaned down to see a man standing in the entry. No waiting for a buildup of nerves. Fear injected itself straight into my veins.

I swallowed a scream. *God help me! What do I do now?* Maybe while the stranger went into another part of the house, I could sneak out.

2

THAT FLOCK OF WILLIES

Suddenly the stranger turned around and said "Hello" in the most innocent voice imaginable. "Miss Bailey? Is that your car? I'm here on behalf of your grandmother, Minna Short. She gave me a key. I'm supposed to help you get settled."

I could feel the boom-banging of my heart as if it were making up its own new funky beat. I forced in a deep breath and released it slowly to get the organ that seemed to be in charge of my blood to calm down a bit.

Could this mild-mannered guy truly be a cat slayer? And could he be coming back to exterminate me? Just in case, I fumbled with my purse and pulled out my mini-hairspray can that sort of looked like the pepper stuff and held it up like a gun. "If you're lying, then I'll have to spray you with my. . .deadly spray." As I shakily descended a few steps, I saw the most boyishly handsome man I'd ever wrapped my eyes around. Stocky but not fat. Bright, inquisitive face. And good, strong arms. The kind that would work well at hugging on scary-movie nights. Or for holding a child. *Boy, where did that come from? He's probably the local loon, and I already have him as the father of my children!*

The stranger grinned up at me. He rated high on the cute scale even if he were the local loon.

"I have spray. I warn you," I said with more seductive tones than menacing ones.

"Your attorney told me you'd come here tonight, and I'm supposed to make sure you're okay," the stranger said.

"My attorney is a scary man. He wears plaid. I hope you don't work with him."

The stranger looked down at his plaid shirt and chuckled. "No, but I had to deal with him because he was your grandmother's attorney, and I was her Realtor. You know, it might have been easier if you'd come in the daytime."

Was he using a silly tone with me? I came down a few more steps to find out.

"By the way, my girlfriend, Priscilla, has one of those sprays. She says it comes in handy living in Houston. You know, the humidity. . .her hair."

I got so hung up on the word *girlfriend*, I didn't hear much of what the stranger had said. "Does she go by Prissy? I'm sorry. I don't know why I asked that. It's none of my business."

"Are you going to put your weapon down now?" The stranger, who appeared to be in his mid-thirties, at least made an effort to rein in his laughter.

"Sure." I stuffed the can back into my purse and decided to fire some questions at him instead. "But

I would like to know why my grandmother's Realtor would come late at night to make sure I'm *settled*."

"You have a reasonable question there."

"By the way, you scared me out of my gourd earlier. Couldn't you have rung the doorbell?" I asked.

"It's broken. I *did* knock. You left the door ajar, and I heard. . .singing. Very nice singing, I might add."

"Oh. I was. . .trying to shoo off the willies."

He grinned then. My face betrayed me as I smiled back.

"You know, you really shouldn't leave the door open even though it's a pretty safe neighborhood." He raked his fingers through his hair as if he'd said something that made him uncomfortable. "Listen, I'm sorry I scared you. I just came to help."

"Thank you. But I guess you could have waited until morning."

"I thought the same thing about you. There *are* hotels here."

"It's a long, boring story, I'm afraid." I made my way down the rest of the creaking stairs and joined him in the entry. On closer inspection, I realized the stranger had eyes the color of milk chocolate and thick brown hair that looked sun-highlighted. I noticed it curled a little at the edges. His smile wasn't bad either. I wondered if his grandmother used to pinch his cheeks when he was little. *What am I doing? Maybe I need to get out more.*

"Well, I live in this neighborhood, so it was easy for me to stop in. I guess I should have introduced myself. I'm Maxwell Sumner. People call me Max."

"Max. I'm Bailey Walker." I shook his warm hand, deciding he wasn't the local loon after all.

"Good to meet you, Bailey. Your grandmother talked about you. Often."

"I miss her." I drifted a bit and then shook myself out of my reverie. "By the way, I still don't fully understand why you're here. Aren't you going beyond the call of duty? I'm a Realtor, too, and I never do this." I wiped my perspiring hands on my capris. "I guess what I'm really trying to say is if you're hoping I'll use you as a Realtor to sell this place, I'm not interested. I'm sorry." *Was I too blunt?*

"No. That's not why I'm here." He put his weight on one foot and then the other. "I think you'd better sit down. There's more to the story."

I decided to chance sitting on the living room couch. The ratty thing looked like it had used up all of its good days *and* bad days. I couldn't help looking around and wondering how I would ever make this archaeological dig into something livable. Oh well. *Focus on the matter at hand, Bailey.*

Maxwell stood by the fireplace with his hands jammed into his pockets. "Your grandmother set up something special for you." He seemed to read my expression. "Your grandmother hired me right before she died to sort of. . .

watch out for you. I had no intention of telling you this tonight, because you need to get settled in."

"Well, this certainly wasn't expected." I didn't know whether to laugh or cry at his proposal. "Does that mean I'm a toddler in need of a nanny?" I raised an eyebrow.

"I can assure you that's not what I had in mind."

"Well, what *do* you have in mind exactly?" I asked, thinking how I felt cornered.

"Tell you what. I'll take you out for a businesslike lunch tomorrow, and I'll tell you everything you want to know. I'll even bring Priscilla if that would make you feel more at ease."

"If you're not too tired, I'd like to know now," I said.

Max clamped his hand at the back of his neck and rubbed his muscles as if he had a headache. When our eyes met, I had my hand in the same position, also massaging my neck. Both of us nearly laughed, but we let it go.

"All right. I'll tell you now," Max said. "Your grandmother isn't paying me to watch over you for the rest of your life." His stare took on a new level of gravity. "I'm being paid a small amount out of a unique trust fund to make sure you're okay. . .until you find a. . .husband."

"So you're not my nanny. You're my matchmaker?" I think my gray eyes got really big about then. Could this surprise be worse than the dead cat?

"I wouldn't put it that way. I certainly won't be

lining up dates for you, but I'm to make sure you're okay until you. . .marry. Then my job is done."

I folded my arms around my middle to calm myself. "Granny always got the last laugh. I tell you, I loved her dearly, but this is a little weird. Isn't it? I mean, how did you come to agree to do such a thing? I hope you won't be offended if I ask if you're the type who feeds off rich old women."

"I would ask the same question if I were you. I did say no to your grandmother quite a few times, but she could be very persistent."

"Well, yes, at times, that was quite true," I said.

Maxwell shook his head and chuckled. "You know your grandmother loved buying quirky homes." He glanced around. "Although, she bought this house decades ago, before I was even born. She sold all her houses toward the end of her life, as I'm sure you know—except for this one. She wanted you to have it."

"Yes, I know." I paused noticeably, wanting to change the subject. "By the way, if you don't mind, could we explore that original topic some more? If you're not my nanny or my matchmaker, then what exactly will you be?" I asked.

"I guess you could think of me as a brother-type person who watches out for you."

"Did my grandmother tell you I'm kind of a private-type person who might not *want* a stranger checking up on me all the time?" I asked.

"Yes. She mentioned it. And she wanted to help you work through it."

"Work through it?" I rose to my feet. "You make it sound like it's something I need counseling for." *Oh dear. I think I added too much edge in my voice just then.*

"You know, I liked your grandmother. She was a good woman, and I sincerely want to honor what she asked me to do. But I won't argue with you or make a nuisance of myself. So, I'll leave your key on the mantle." Maxwell walked back toward the entryway. "A word of warning: There's quite a congregation of bats in the attic in case you go up there tomorrow. And they won't be singing hymns. Do be careful."

"Are there snakes, too?" I asked, wondering if he now had some scare tactics up his sleeve.

"I saw several snakes in the woodpile just outside the kitchen door, but they're not the poisonous kind."

"Really?" I asked, losing another chunk of my cocky attitude and hurrying to follow him to the front door.

"And maybe you haven't noticed yet, but I see you've got some nasty cuts on your legs. I'd clean those up with some peroxide tonight."

I looked down at my shins and was surprised to see streaks of blood. I sighed and said, "I think the weeds are guilty. They had knives."

A chuckle escaped Max's mouth, and then he grew

serious again. "I'm sorry. That's my fault. I had someone mow and clean up the back, but apparently he didn't get around to the front." He cleared his throat.

"No problem." I played the patient game. I could be mighty wrong, but this Max guy seemed to be stalling for some reason.

"Well, there's a leak in the master bedroom ceiling right above your mattress, the back door is loose on its hinges, and the floor is rotten up on the west side of the third floor. Those things would have been fixed, but you got here before I could see to them." He grinned for no apparent reason. "And the house does moan at night. No walking souls, just creaky joints in a really old house. I had the utilities turned on for you, and there's a new phone hooked up in the kitchen. I pray all goes well for you. You'll need it in *this* old house. I'll leave my card on the entry table. . .for *when* you change your mind."

"Thank you for coming." *Hmm. So, this is how the offender got in—a back door loose on its hinges.*

Max picked up an umbrella by the door. "And. . . I'm curious about something."

"Yes?" Why did he keep staring at me?

"Aren't you afraid to stay here by yourself tonight?"

I crossed my arms. "Why do you ask?" I felt a tremor run through me.

"Oh, I don't know. Just a question. I have five younger sisters. And you couldn't pay any one of them enough to stay alone in this old house at night. . . especially during a thunderstorm."

"Well, I've been through a lot these last few years. I guess sometimes life forces us to toughen up. . .even if we don't want to."

"Your grandmother said you were amazing. I think I agree."

"By the way, I have a question for you, too," I said.

"Fair enough."

"How do you feel about. . .cats?" I watched closely for his reaction.

He laughed. "I guess they're okay. Come to think of it, you might want to get one in case there're rats around."

"Rats?" Somehow now I wished I hadn't asked. "Okay. Thanks."

Then, as in an old movie, Max gave me a two-fingered salute. "Well then, good night. . .Miss Walker."

"Good-bye. And thanks." I started to slip and say, "Wait, don't go. . .somebody's trying to frighten me out of my wits." But Max had already slipped out the door.

Had he said "thunderstorm"? All at once, lightning hurled itself through the windows like shards of broken glass. I jumped at the thunderclap even though I had sensed it coming.

Oh great. This is just great. A storm. Rain. I remembered Max mentioning a leak in the master bedroom. I double-locked the front door, shoved a piece of heavy furniture in front of the back door, and then trudged back up the stairs with my suitcase. This time I made up my own tune to shoo that flock of willies away. My mind played with the idea of hidden creatures waiting to pounce, but I allowed Max to occupy the rest of the space in my head. His manner had been charming and kind. And his sunny grins had been like a soft light in this dark cellar of a house.

But a haunting notion nudged its way into my reverie. *Wasn't their agreement rather bizarre? Whose idea had it really been to watch over me? Could he have gotten close enough to Granny's finances to embezzle from her, and now he thought I was wealthy, too?* My hand shook as it covered my mouth. Granny had always been so robust until that strange illness. Maybe she'd been tricked into signing over her money to him and then murdered.

Lightning slashed through the house again, making me shudder. *What am I thinking?* Max seemed like a decent sort, and Granny trusted him. I'm going to toss that preposterous notion out the window where it belongs.

There. I'd almost made it to the second floor, and I was still alive. Just as I celebrated that milestone, I stumbled on the last step, bumping my head on the railing. Lightning flared around me and my poor aching head like a strobe light.

BEYOND SHABBY CHIC

I flicked another switch. Light flooded the hallway on the second floor. *I will never take electricity for granted again.* But, in spite of my victories over the darkness, my head throbbed more than ever, and by now, my demure glow had blossomed into a beastly sweat. But that was simple mud-pie play compared to the manure-pit realization I would now have to accept: no central air or any kind of window units in the house. How would I survive the heat? This could be serious.

I dragged myself from room to room, checking out the bedrooms and baths on the second floor. So far, they were empty and monster-free, but they were also dreary and dripping in ancient smells. *Not a bad floor plan, though.*

I reached in to turn on the light in the last room, thinking it must be the master bedroom, but once I saw it, I realized it should be called the master chamber of horrors. The overhead light revealed furniture that had gone light-years beyond shabby chic. The brass bed had a mattress that looked as though it'd been used for a barricade in one of the world wars. And the two stuffed chairs could have accessorized any abandoned fridge on somebody's front lawn. A bulb sort of dangled, prisonlike, above the bed. Even with all the junk, the room possessed a starkness. . .a spectacle of nothingness. *Yes, this house certainly had an abundance of that.*

I dropped my stuff down with a thud. Was that an echo? I then noticed a noisy stalactite-like drip coming from the ceiling down to the mattress. Oh great. Max had been telling the truth. The mattress reeked damp and mold even though it hadn't turned green. Yet. "No way I'm sleeping on *that* thing tonight," I said aloud, hoping no one was around to counter my exclamation.

Well, now I'm down to two choices. Since there weren't any other beds, I'd have to pick either the couch in the living room or this bedroom floor for my sleeping accommodations. Hmm. I felt almost positive the couch housed living things—perhaps a legion of dust mites that could carry me off on their backs in the night. The floor suddenly looked pretty good to me. I was tough.

I stomped around the bed. At least the boards didn't seem rotten. Perhaps the mattress had absorbed the moisture, thus saving the floor. "Okay, there's one good thing to put on my blessing list." I balled my hand into a fist to get it to stop shaking.

On the opposite wall, two bare and darkened windows stared at me like vacant eye sockets. I wondered if in the night my fear tank might get so full I'd go screaming out into the darkness with my nightgown flowing, like on the covers of those gothic novels I'd read as a teenager. I remembered that a light always illuminated a top window as if declaring something menacing had come calling.

Since my windows were bare, the neighbors could see every single move I made. I moaned. I'd have to stumble around in the dark or sleep in my clothes tonight. Considering I felt too tired to peel off my garments, I opted for the latter.

On the wall to my right, I saw a lone closet door. Cringing at the thought of what might be behind closed doors, I yanked it open in one swift motion. I discovered the fast-pull method was better on creaky doors than the maddeningly slow kind that allows for an unnecessary build-up of nervous heart palpitations.

The closet appeared empty except for a three-legged table. As I reached for it, I bumped the edge, causing it to fall against the back of the closet. Even the bang against the wall sounded unnatural and lonely. I quickly shook myself free of those musings and carried the table over to the bed to use as a nightstand. I then opened my suitcase to set up my tiny world.

First, I rolled out a blanket and then pulled out a small pillow from my suitcase—the one with my favorite chubby cherub pillowcase. The floor would be unforgiving on the bones of a thirty-year-old woman, but I felt so tired, I could probably get to sleep on a bed of finely sharpened pencils. Pointed up. I lifted out a small marble clock of Granny's as well as her favorite Bible and a small sack of seeds from her garden. Then I took out the framed photos of my parents and one of Granny. I traced their faces with my fingers.

I touched the diamond necklace around my neck. A gift from Granny just to say she loved me and was proud of me. *I will never sell this necklace, even if I have to eat tuna for the rest of my life.* And tuna and I hadn't been on eating terms in years.

Gazing into my suitcase, I pulled out a small stack of mystery novels and then my lovely music box. Hand-carved mahogany with inlaid gold. The name of its sweet tune was unknown to me, but the melody always transported me to a peaceful and whimsical place. Fairies came to life in magical grasses deep in the woods of my imagination. It was a place where the child in me could go and play without worry or regret.

Even though my melodious box always coaxed a smile from me, all I could muster tonight was a sigh. "Oh, Granny, I miss you."

Yes, she'd been such a sweet riot, but I'd loved what my mom had always said about her. "Your granny is very special," she'd say with a wink. "She's full of angel stuffings." I remembered that when Granny's heart stopped beating, the sun went behind the clouds that day and stayed there, as if all the earth had mourned her passing, too.

I wound up the key to let the notes play again. My stomach emitted an angry rumble. I looked down. There sat my last chocolate treat, the one that camouflaged itself as a power-protein bar. On tearing open the wrapper, I could see it had entered the liquefy-and-flow stage. So instead of munching, my tongue sort of licked its way around the paper. Oh well. What else could go wrong? I'd covered about everything.

I gave the key on the music box a few more twists. Its tinkling melody consumed some of the loneliness of the house. Fortunately, the thunder had gone off to terrorize someone else, and so except for sputtering rain, the night had quieted itself. When my music box wound down, I suddenly noticed the drip again. Splat. Spit. Splat. Like some kind of water torture. *Okay, so how am I going to sleep?* I stuffed in a pair of foam earplugs I'd kept in my purse. Silence filled my head. Good. Now I wouldn't have to set up my belongings in another room.

Out of the blue, I remembered Granny Minna telling me about her most potent nightmare. In fact, she talked about it often. In her dream, she'd be trapped in a vacant house, and the only way out was through a spider-lined passage. In fact, that passage had been in the closet of the master bedroom in an old house not unlike this one. But what always made Granny's eyes twinkle was when she told of the treasure that was hidden inside. Then she'd always give me an exaggerated wink.

At that moment a wild thought flitted across my brain. I had indeed heard a strange and hollow sound when the night table bumped the back of the closet. My imagination had obviously taken on heights of screenplay proportions. "But what if Granny had repeated those stories to me for a reason?"

4

RODENTIAL QUALITIES

What a hoot. I laughed out loud in my now muffled, plugged-up world. Enough fictional nonsense. I closed the bedroom door to keep out any stray bats and settled down onto my makeshift bed. I suppose I needed to wash my face and clean up for the night, but my body gave me the thumbs down. So, I closed my eyes and waited for any drowsy sensations. None came. None at all. I thought maybe making a mental to-do list might help me. *Get cleaning supplies and an air mattress tomorrow. Buy peanut butter, bread, baby carrots, apples, and milk.* Just enough money left to live on while finding a job. Oh, and I needed to locate a nearby Laundromat until I could afford a washer and dryer. *Okay, not sleepy yet.*

Like flipping pancakes, I tried my usual tossing and turning, but every movement felt painful against the unforgiving floor. Surely exhaustion would force me to sleep. I waited again. Nothing. The thumping of my heart seemed to be more noticeable now. *Oh great.* My own heartbeat was going to keep me awake.

After a few minutes of scanning the floor for rodential qualities and trying to get my mind off the person who'd presented me with a dead cat, my muscles finally relaxed. I began to drift into that land of drawbridges, where the brain lowers its defenses and escorts in a whole motley crew of fantasies and fears.

I could see the sleepies riding in on horses. They waved at me as they passed by. Then somewhere deep inside I heard an echoing, like someone lost in a cave calling for help. The word "hollow" rose and fell in the air. Was I hollow? What did it mean? Did I say the words out loud? Or was someone else talking?

Oh, to float in that state of half-awareness and drifty bliss. Where was I? Something touched my face. Bat wings? God help me. My eyes squinted open. Why had the room gotten so bright? Light everywhere. *Where am I? Who am I?*

A human in a fairy costume shook my arm. "Dear heart, I see you breathing. But you're scaring me. Are you okay? Wake up."

Real words from a real person! My mind jolted to attention. I forced my eyes open and saw a big face in my face. My lungs upchucked a scream. A really loud one. The kind of scream you hear in movies when they film from a distance as flocks of birds flutter away. Then the scream fills the atmosphere. The earth stops its rotation. And the whole audience cringes.

The big face jumped back and let out a big noise that sounded just like mine. Then I screamed again. I knew who I was and where I was now, so I yanked out my earplugs. "Who *are* you?" I asked a little more sharply than intended.

The face—that of a woman—stared at me as if not knowing whether to talk or laugh. "Hi. I'm Dedra Morgan. Guess we got into a screaming jag there. Are you okay?" The brown-eyed woman leaned down and fanned my face. "I thought maybe you were dead. We had that happen about a year ago in this neighborhood. A woman several doors down died in her home because nobody was watching out for her. Now we're all a little overprotective. Sorry."

Was that brown-eyed woman still talking? I sat up against the bed and groaned. "I don't think I'm dead." I rubbed my neck and stretched my aching back. "But you scared me, too."

"Sorry about that. I mean no harm," Dedra said stiffly, like an alien who had just landed. "I'm just a neighbor." She stood tall, giving me the scout's honor sign.

For a moment, I ignored the uninvited stranger and concentrated on my ailing body. "I feel like I've been asleep for years." I considered her words. "Why did you think I might be dead?"

"Well, it's noon, and when you didn't come to the door, I got worried. And then when I saw you here on the floor, I called your name and you didn't move. At all. Must have been the earplugs," Dedra said.

"I must have slept on my arm. *Oww.*" In fact, my arm

felt as though it'd been attached to somebody else's body. I kept slapping it, trying to get the blood pumping again. My flesh came alive as if bitten by a million chomping ants. After a groan, I considered the bizarreness of the situation. "Do you mind if I ask how you got in?"

Dedra chuckled and flipped her long black curls over her shoulder. "Oh that. Max gave me a key. We wanted to make sure you were okay. I'm sorry for scaring you. And I realize barging in like this is really *not* kosher, but one gets an imagination concerning this house."

"And why's that?" I asked, wondering what kind of house I'd really inherited.

"Nothing too sinister." Dedra raised her hands. "I'm so glad you're okay."

I rubbed my eyes and wiped my sweaty bangs off my forehead. *Noon. I had so much stuff I needed to do today.* I think my brain had sidestepped some bit of information. Yes! "You mean Max. . .Sumner actually gave you a key?" I couldn't believe it. The nerve. I wondered how many copies he'd passed out before he gave it back to me. Apparently this Max character wasn't going to give up easily. I should be angry, but I felt too knocked out of sync to know for sure what to do next. I dropped the earplugs onto the table. "I don't usually wear these at night, but there was a pesky drip in here."

"Yeah. It's a really old house, but it's a good one. Worth keeping and fixing up. Max says so, and he knows houses." Dedra touched the decorative trim around the door and sighed. "Yes, lots of character. Hey, how about some coffee?"

"You brought me coffee? You don't even know me."

"No, but a neighbor can do that for another neighbor. I live next door. I have the beige house with the green shutters."

"I'm afraid I didn't notice too much last night. I was a zombie."

Dedra handed me one of the steaming coffees from the table. "Cream, no sugar. Just the way you like it."

"Yeah. I guess this *is* the way I like it. But how did you know?" *People around here seem to know more about me than I do.*

"Max told me," Dedra said.

"I feel like I'm still dreaming. I only just met this Max guy last night, so how would he—"

"Max is an exceptional kind of guy. He notices a lot even when you think he's not paying attention. Most men do just the opposite. They pretend to listen, and then later you realize they don't have a clue about what you said."

"Sorry, I'm still confused here," I said. "It was late last night, and believe me, I didn't talk coffee with Max Sumner. So how—"

"Well, Max found out somehow." Dedra shrugged her shoulders and drank from her cup. "That's sooo good. Really hits the spot, doesn't it?"

I turned the smooth cup around to the tiny spout. The coffee aroma teased my senses, so I sipped on my beverage even though our little soiree seemed pretty weird. But considering the delicious scent wafting from the cup, I guess I would have accepted it from the hand of Dr. Jekyll. After a couple of silent swigs, I said, "Wait a minute. I still feel like I'm missing something here. How do you know Max?"

"Max and I dated for a while. . .years ago. It didn't work out." Dedra's slender figure glided to the floor as her frothy skirt billowed around her in gentle waves. She adjusted her denim vest and settled down into a comfortable position as if she were staying for a good long spell. "I think Max is marvelous in every way. But I can tell he just wants to be friends." She smiled. "It's okay. I've learned to deal with it."

Even though Dedra was grinning, there was something else lingering in her expression. She must still have feelings for Max. I hadn't even been in my house one full day, and I was already embroiled in the personal travails of the neighbors. *Oh brother.* And I still didn't feel okay with my new neighbor popping over with her key to my house. I took another sip of the steaming coffee to calm down. "This *is* good. Thanks."

"You're welcome. By the way, you have a red spot on your forehead. Are you okay? It looks kind of swollen. Do you need some first-aid? I've got a few supplies at the house."

I touched my bump. "*Oww.* Yeah, it's still sore, but I'll live. I bumped my head on the railing last night. But I think my back is in a lot worse shape for sleeping on the floor."

"I have an air mattress and some sheets you can borrow until you get all set up. By the way, Max told me some about your grandmother and this house."

I wondered who else Max had told.

Dedra prattled on about this and that as if she were holding a conversation with herself.

My mind drifted.

Dedra went on chatting while she twiddled with her frothy peasant sleeves. "My two dearest friends moved away this year. I'm in need of a friend. You seem about my age. Maybe thirty."

Good guess. She paused to wait for my response, so I nodded.

"Perhaps this is an unexpected blessing. . .you moving here."

Did this woman expect me to gush? We'd barely met. I started to feel a little pressed in, so I didn't respond to her comment.

Dedra played with her long Roaring-'20s-style strand of pearls while we sat in silence.

"I don't know what to say," I finally said. "I'm just so used to doing stuff solo."

Dedra smiled. The black curly hair that framed her oval face made her look cherublike. But angel or not,

I knew she'd be the clingy type. I'd seen them before. And I didn't cope well with people like that. Still, I didn't want to come off like a total social misfit. "We'll see how it goes." Then I thought of the package from the previous night. "I was just wondering something, Dedra. How do you feel about. . .cats?" I felt a stab of guilt once the words had escaped my mouth.

"That was kind of random." Dedra's eyebrows came together. "Why would you ask me that?"

"Never mind." I shook my head. "Sorry." The idea of this woman calculatingly suffocating a cat seemed ludicrous. And yet she did have a key.

Dedra shrugged. "I'll see ya later, gator." She twirled out the door." Then she popped her head back in. "By the way, two things. Just before I shook you awake, you said the word *hollow*. Should that mean anything? And in case no one told you, your house has a name. Volstead Manor. It's probably the name of the people who built it ages ago." Before I could say anything, she headed down the hall in her thin rubber shoes, flip-flapping all the way.

I sat there stupefied. Volstead Manor. Why did that name sound faintly familiar? Hmm. Then I remembered I should have asked Dedra for my house key back. *Oh well. I'm sure she'll be back.*

I wound up my music box for company. Tiny notes cheered the air as the word *Volstead* danced around in my head.

I tasted the coffee again. Some kind of rich, dark blend. *Mmm.* But in spite of the coffee, the facts still stormed around me—a female cyclone named Dedra had just blown into my house with her own personal key to my world, and a man whom I didn't know had made it his business to manipulate my life. Oh, and some maniac was trying to force me out of my house. *Not a good start to a quiet life in Houston, eh, Bailey?*

As the caffeine cleared the cobwebs out of my head, my plan unfolded on how to extricate myself from the claustrophobic and potentially dangerous situation I'd found myself in. First, I would be watchful with Dedra. Not because she was a cat killer, but because I wasn't ready for any close friendships. She certainly seemed nice, but I knew how the story would go. There'd be the pajama-party giddy phase with the plethora of gooey feelings, praises, sharpened listening skills, fresh humor, cute girly cards, and a bonding of such hyperbolic proportions it would blow all reality out of the water.

I took another slurp of my coffee and wondered why relationships always seem to have the same pattern. Maybe expectations were just too high. Yes, that was it. People try, but life gets messy and tedious. People change. Relationships get trampled. And then other times, irritations build up like smelly cigarette butts in an ashtray. Not very appealing.

Back to my plan. Second, I would deal with Max

the same way. Approach with caution. Third, I would bury the poor kitty, fix the back door, and look for any traces that might lead to the person who'd broken into my house. A solid plan always made me feel in control again.

I dragged myself off the floor into an upright position. I didn't know I had that many muscles to throb. *This is misery. I'm also going to buy an air mattress. I don't need to borrow Dedra's things. I need my own stuff.*

I tried to take another drink of my beverage, but realized my cup was empty. Made me think of what Dedra mentioned. I'd said the word *hollow*. Did I dream about something hollow? I flicked my fingers in rapid fire to help me think. Of course. How could I forget? Granny's nightmare. I was going to check out that hollow sound inside the closet. *I'll give myself one more childish indulgence before I face the music.*

Trying not to get too excited, I sashayed into the closet with the flashlight in hand. I picked up my shoe and tapped the heel along the wainscoting. How odd. Who puts oak wainscoting inside a closet? A little over the top. *Okay, concentrate, Bailey. Tap, tap, tap.* Solid. Moving along. *Tap, tap, tap.* Solid. *Tap.* Something else. Like a vacant sound. I'd been right. *Forget the whys and the debutante attitude, Bailey. Just go for it.* I hammered the area with my heel and ran my hands along the trim with more enthusiasm. Sure enough, one large square area echoed a different sound from the rest of the wall.

As I paid more attention to the trim board along the top of the wainscoting, I noticed it wasn't continuous. There were breaks that outlined a section of wood that appeared to be about three-feet by three-feet. My hands perspired as my heart rate increased.

I tugged up on the lacquered trim with my fingertips. Nothing budged. My shoulders sagged. What in the world was I doing? Chasing silly notions like an adolescent when I had much more important things to do? But somehow I couldn't give up. I dried the sweat from my hands and got a firmer grip on the edge. Nothing. I pounded on the trim in case it needed some loosening up. I yanked again. Just as I began to wallow in some shame, I heard a noise. A slight movement, like wood settling back on wood. I must have dislodged something. With renewed vigor, I grabbed under the trim again, straining my poor fingers and wrists until they ached.

A square section of the boards suddenly lifted up like a sliding door. When it rolled all the way up, it locked into place with a pronounced thud. *Wow. Certainly a more sophisticated system than I'd ever imagined.*

Air, like cooling eddies, flowed around my ankles. Particles of dust churned up around me. I coughed and put my shirt over my mouth. I stepped forward, aiming my light down into a hole. *Dark as a cavern.* A new breed of odors attacked my senses—a musty smell with a dose of something acidic. Like vinegar.

Tremors coursed through my hands, making the light jiggle. *Come on, Bailey. Calm yourself.* I got on my knees for a closer look and stopped the light on some boards just below me. Some two-by-four pieces of wood had been nailed to the side of the passage every foot or so. The boards created a crude kind of ladder, which appeared quite precarious. *Boy, I bet I never go down that ladder.*

As I looked straight into the hole, I spotted a wall about three feet away. I leaned in farther, taking note that the distance from side to side was roughly ten feet. But the bottom was nowhere in sight, which possibly meant the passage went the full length of the two stories. In other words, it would be a long way to fall.

Spiderwebs crisscrossed the channel. Incredible. Just like the long narrow passage Granny had always talked about.

Hmm. There must be a bedroom on the other side. That meant the passage had probably been designed into the house when it was built. My heart raced with the thrill of discovery. But did Granny have the dream because of this door? Had she found it, too? Or was this some strange coincidence? I would never know, but it was still a remarkable find.

I pointed the flashlight straight ahead of me into the black space and saw a strange sight. Of all the things I imagined in a secret place like this, I never have would guessed what I saw hidden there.

5

THE TINY TEMPEST

Glass jars—rows of them—sat on wooden shelves, entombed in dust like buried relics. They were old canning jars. Unlabeled. The light revealed some sort of transparent liquid in a few of them. *How odd. Now why would anyone go to so much trouble to hide something so innocuous?* I meticulously scanned the passage with my flashlight, guiding the beam up and down. The light revealed more shelving but fewer jars.

I wanted a closer examination of the containers, so I decided to go for it. I sat the flashlight in the top rung of the ladder so it kept a continuous spray of light where I wanted to reach. I lowered myself onto my side and then scooted partially over the hole, all the time keeping a white-knuckled grip on the sliding door frame behind me.

Amid my squirming, I accidentally knocked a nail into the dark cavity. I waited. Finally, I heard a clinking sound as metal hit stone. Guess I'd need to be careful. My bones wouldn't fare so well.

I leaned over the abyss. *Careful, Bailey. One slip and you'll be forced to wear one of those scenic hospital gowns that opens in the back.* Or perhaps much worse.

I scooted out a bit more and then stretched my arm to the goal. Just an inch or two more. Almost got a jar. *Come on, Bailey. You can do it.* I tightened my grip on the frame behind me, which sent sharp pains through my wrist and fingers. With my other hand, I latched onto one of the jars as I tried to ignore the tickling spiderwebs. Good hold. Got it. I tried pulling myself back up, but my body twisted. My strength wavered, and my hand wanted to let go. I breathed and then prayed. *Do it now.* In one aching lunge, I pulled myself and the jar safely out of the hole.

Whew. I sat down on the floor, rubbing my wrist. After a brief recovery, my attention honed in on my discovery. I wiped off the dust and spiderwebs from the jar and shook the contents. I stared at the tiny tempest I'd made inside. The fluid looked like water as it sloshed around and sparkled in the light. *But why would anyone hide jars of water?*

I tried the top. Stuck. I tapped the rim against the inside of the door panel and tried it again. The lid started to give way, making a gritty sound as I turned it. Finally, I lifted the top off and took a deep sniff of the contents. The stinging smell of strong liquor stung my nose. Oh my. *Of course. Now I remember.* Granny said the house had been built in the late '20s. Prohibition. *This is moonshine.* The folks who'd lived here years ago weren't canning up their garden veggies; they were concealing their bootlegging business! Now *there's* some interesting history about the house. I sat there thinking about the angles and implications of this information. And whom would I tell? Not sure.

Maybe some more exploration was in order. I decided to shine the flashlight just below me. I noticed three gallon jars on an empty shelf, and they appeared to be full of something green. Funny. They looked like bills. Dollar bills. Were they counterfeit? Or was it real money from their illegal business?

I moved in even closer with the light. A guy who looked like Benjamin Franklin stared back at me on those bills. Wasn't he on the one-hundred-dollar bill? Lots of these new green bills filled the jars. But they couldn't be real. Could they? With my curiosity scampering now like hamsters on espresso, I decided to reach for one of the three big jars full of the green.

I dropped down on my belly and with amazing ease, lifted one of the gallon jars up onto the floor next to me.

I wiped the perspiration dripping from my face and then tried unscrewing the shiny new lid. It opened easily as if it hadn't been there long. I picked out one of the bills and studied it. Franklin's portrait adorned the bill, and it looked amazingly real. I saw an envelope below a few of the bills and opened it. A folded letter fell out. I took the note into the bedroom, lowered myself on a nearby chair, and began to read.

My dear Bailey,
Surprise! It was my last wish on this earth

that you, Bailey Marie Walker, would find these three gallon jars of money, which I placed here after I found out I was ill. I've never told a soul about this money—not even my attorney, Mr. Lakes.

Invest wisely, my dearest, and if you choose to fix up this old house, you should have plenty of extra funds. You'll find it to be a house full of mysteries, but one I also think you will come to enjoy with a full heart.

By the time you read this, I will have had time to talk to my sweet Jesus, and I will be well and whole again. Rejoice with me! But remember, weeping over a loss is okay, too. Even Jesus did. If God hadn't expected us to cry from time to time, he wouldn't have given us tear ducts.

Now, before I took off on my journey, I prayed you'd have a long life, surrounded by the finest treasures, which are a strong faith, good friends, and if God wills it, a Christian man who'll bring you even more years of happiness and some little ones, too!

Always talk to the One who created you. Even when things seem too dark or too impossible. He's the God of redemption and of love. In fact, He's watching out for you, even now.

So, dearie, on this other matter of moneys,
these three jars should contain half a million
dollars. I don't need it now! Have a good life, and
I'll see you in heaven when the time is right! I love
you, my dearest child.

Your Granny Minna.

I paused for a moment. My heart constricted into a ball of pain. I felt the anguish of losing Granny all over again, and yet I also felt gratitude for the love message. I read the letter again, more carefully this time, holding on to every phrase and thinking of every nuance of her words. My granny had written me one last letter. *Thank you, God.* I kissed the note and slid it gently into the drawer of my music box.

I turned around to stare at the gallon jar, my eyes widening with the realization of what it meant. Half a million dollars. It was like a dream, only I knew I was wide awake. I wasn't sure what to do first. Well, maybe I did know. I thanked God, and then realized I didn't have to use my lunch money for cleaning supplies. I now had money for both. It was certainly more than I'd asked God for.

I laughed out loud, wondering if this moment made God chuckle, too. And then I had this need to share my good news with someone. But I had no one to tell. I guess that's the way things are when one chooses to drift through life on an empty barge.

Suddenly, I couldn't help letting out a couple of whoops. The cheer bounced around the room and echoed back to me, reminding me to share the news with someone. I hadn't experienced so many different emotions in a long time. My sensory catchall felt like an overflowing tub. I couldn't keep up. I barely knew how to act.

Granny had always been one who loved divvying out surprises, but I hadn't expected this. I'd already been willed a marble clock, her favorite Bible, a huge set of Fostoria dishes, and seeds from her garden. It had been enough to remember her by. But this gift! This was too much. I looked around the room. Well, maybe not. The house did need tons of work, and somehow now, I really did want to stay. More than ever the house seemed like a memory of Granny, and that made all the difference.

My mind raced forward, making even more plans. This would be enough money to invest, as well as to fix up the house. It would buy me some time to make this house into a home before I started another full-time job. I liked the sound of that. I think God did, too.

I went back to the passage and pulled up the other two money jars. I hid all the containers in the corner of my closet and then yanked down the sliding door. After plopping onto one of the stuffed chairs, I touched my upturned lips with my fingertips. Smiles had such a good feel to them. They'd been unfamiliar for too long.

I headed to the bathroom. Maybe I could do my morning routine without touching anything. Later, when I climbed into some clean jeans and a T-shirt, I heard a pounding. *What's that?* The front door. Dedra again? As I headed downstairs, I glanced around. *Wow. I still can't believe I own this huge place.* I checked the peephole thoroughly and then opened the door.

Dedra stood on my porch with a daisy stuck in her hair like a flower child. Her arms strained with every kind of cleaning supply within the known galaxy. "Well, how about we wash some of the dirt off this old house and see what secrets we find."

Incredible. Dedra had no idea how right she was. The bootleggers had to hide their wares or risk jail. The house had to be bursting with stories to tell. Suddenly, I wanted to just blurt out all of the news of Granny's money to Dedra, but it just didn't seem like the right time. "Are you sure you want to help me?"

Dedra stepped into the entry. "Max would have liked to have helped us today, but—"

"I wouldn't expect him to drive all the way over here." I took some of the supplies from her arms.

Dedra's face radiated confusion with a hint of amusement. "Didn't you know? Max is our neighbor. He lives on the other side of me."

6

TOWARD THE EDGE

Mortified. Yes, that summarized my sensibilities about now. A sizzling grenade had just landed on all my good news. As I waited for some kind of internal explosion, I synchronized my vocal cords again to force out the words, "Max Sumner lives only two doors down from me?"

"Yes. Didn't he tell you?"

"Well, I guess he might have said he lived *somewhere* in the neighborhood. But it was late. I was tired. And I thought he was talking generically. Like maybe he resided somewhere on this side of the Continental Divide. I had no—"

"He's a good man."

"Oh, I'm sure." I wished now I'd bothered to look at his business card. "It's just. . .well. . .I'm surprised." *Great. Another unexpected turn of events.* I wondered if Max would use binoculars to make sure I met a two-dates-per-weekend quota. Or maybe he'd constantly be knocking on the door wanting some kind of matrimonial updates. What else would happen today? I sensed a strange pull of some kind, like a toy boat headed toward the edge of Niagara. Whatever. I decided I might as well spill some information since I was about to topple over the edge. "Dedra. I have something I want to tell you. Good news." I had her sit down on the couch for support. "Well, earlier when you left for a while. . .I found something in the house."

"Like what?" Dedra leaned in with more interest than I expected.

"You're not going to believe this. I hardly believe it myself." I paused. Somewhere I heard a drum roll. "My granny Minna left me half a million dollars in cash. I found it up on the second floor behind a closet. The money had been stashed in three gallon-sized jars. Can you believe it? All in one-hundred-dollar bills."

Dedra dropped the bottle of window cleaner from her hand. "Okay, now that is so truly. . .truly amazing. Truly."

I smiled, relieved that she showed genuine surprise with the news, which meant she hadn't known about the money. *And that's a good thing, since Dedra has a key to my house.*

"Mind-boggling, actually. To find something like that in your bedroom," Dedra said.

"Yes." I licked my lips. *Had I mentioned I'd found the money in my bedroom, or was she just good at guessing?* The tiniest shiver ran through me. Then I laughed at myself.

Dedra hugged me. "It's fantastical. But your grandmother was really taking a chance, wasn't she? I mean, what if somebody else had found the money?"

"Well, that would have been difficult since the money was hidden in the wall."

"You mean, like a secret place?" Dedra asked.

I wasn't sure how much to tell her about the passage, so I just nodded. "By the way, for now, please don't tell anyone about this. Okay?"

"I understand," Dedra said. "You know, it might be wise to put your money in the bank. Actually, mine isn't far from here, and they're open."

"Good idea," I said. "And then I guess on Monday it'd be great to have a cleaning crew come so I could concentrate on all the repairs. So, you and I don't really have to clean. But there is something you could help me with."

"Name it."

I threw a tiny piece of my caution to the wind as I said, "Well, you could come with me to the bank. Maybe you can help me convince them that I didn't steal all this cash."

We both laughed.

"Done. And after the bank, we need to shop for a real bed and mattress," Dedra said. "And some little air conditioning units until you can get central air." She held her hands up dramatically. "*And* you need a beta fish."

"Oh. A beta fish?" I asked weakly.

"You know. For company. It's an awfully big house." Dedra clapped her hands together. "And to save time for a little while, you don't need to shop for groceries. Just have food delivered. Then you can make phone calls and get set up."

"That's good. I like that."

Dedra rose from the couch and looked around. "You know, now you'll be able fix this house up. Make it a home. . .or sell it."

I was surprised at her second suggestion but chose to ignore it. After some planning, we locked the house and headed out. The tellers at the bank had to call the head honchos down from upstairs so they could burble and stare like marmosets. I couldn't blame them. They simply had never seen anyone bring in half a million dollars in gallon jugs before. But in the end, the bank took Granny's money with a vigorous handshake, depositing it into a savings account until I could consult with a financial planner.

Dedra and I left the bank in high spirits. It'd been a day I would hold in my memory forever. The day I found the letter and the love gift from Granny and the day I reconsidered the concept of friendship. Maybe.

By seven o'clock that evening, I had a real bed and mattress delivered, one small air conditioner installed in my bedroom, and Dedra's old blankets tacked to the windows. It ranked far from utopia, but I felt a surge of hope.

Once Dedra had gone home, I decided to take on the cheerless job of burying the cat, which I did, laying him to rest in a grave in the far corner of my backyard.

I then checked for traces of anyone breaking into the house or for general mischief. Nothing looked peculiar, except the back door was indeed loose on its hinges, which did seem to make the door easier to force open. After finding a small screwdriver in the garage, I managed to make the door secure again. Maybe whoever had broken in was now finished with their threatening games. I certainly hoped so.

Just as I thought about bedtime, I realized I hadn't checked the third floor tower or attic since I'd moved in, which was pretty crazy since someone could have been lurking up there. How could I have forgotten to check it?

Then I wondered if the bats would be active or gone? Would I fall through the floor up there? Were the decaying boards as mushy as melon rinds? So many questions. Never enough answers. Maybe I could just take a peek before bed. I'd sleep so much better having faced my adversaries and knowing for sure if I could get rid of them soon. But was there such a thing as bat exterminators?

Then a genius of an idea hit me. It would surely win a Great Thinkers Award, if there were such a thing. I picked up my pillow and flashlight and stumbled my way up the staircase to the third floor.

Another closed door. Great. "One, two, three!" I

yelled and jerked the door open. Nothing flew at me. My shoulder relaxed, and I sighed. The third floor consisted of a hallway, enclosed attic spaces, and the little tower.

I turned my attention to the tower and took a quick peek inside. Hmm. What looked like a church steeple from the outside now looked like a square nook on the inside. I liked the idea of windows on each side of the room to give it a sunny atmosphere during the day and a great view by night, but I wasn't so sure about the neighbors being able to see all my activities. Some draperies or blinds might be in order up here too. Yes. It would be a perfect place to make into a reading room for cozying up with a good mystery. But right now, it looked creepy and smelled like fireworks for some odd reason. I shut the door.

Now for the dreaded attic rooms. If I did have bats, I felt somewhat ready to deal with their kind. Yes, I think I had their number. I sensed the bats would be staying out late partying, à la getting loopy on red corpuscle cocktails and maybe watching some old Dracula movies. If that were true, the attic would be ripe for a takeover.

Coming up on the attic door, I didn't sing or utilize my yanking-open-the-door method, but instead I quietly eased it open a crack. I glanced down and saw my T-shirt shaking and almost wished I'd asked Dedra along for moral support. The thought of being a coward egged me on. I prayed for an ounce more courage and opened the door a tiny bit more. Then I saw it. Guano on the floor. Just what I thought. But no bats. At least not from my angle. With my confidence rising, I opened the door and tiptoed inside, searching the rafters for my vinyl-winged friends. None. Yes, indeed, the bats must be out on the town, living it up like bandits.

I realized the time had risen to its fullest to execute my plan. The broken window stood only feet in front of me. *You can do this, Bailey.* So, I strode. I reached. And then I stuffed my pillow in the opening like a cork in an attic bottle. Mission accomplished.

Like a detective who'd just cracked an unsolvable case, I gave a loose-necked nod and grinned. Yes, the bat's sonar would get confused signals, and then they'd fly off dizzily in search for another attic to haunt. My musty, dusty loft was now officially unavailable.

As I exited the scene, I noticed a narrow opening in what appeared to be the underside of the roof. Out of curiosity, I stepped up on a pile of boards and flashed my light into the hole. Someone had created a hiding place by making a fake wall. Clever. *Just how many hiding places did this house have?* A metal tank sat in the space along with some bluish papers. I stacked the loose boards into a mega pile and stepped up higher for a closer look. I tapped the container but couldn't tell what it was, except it had a rounded top and looked quite old. The tank also had a curved pipe coming out of the top like the neck of a swan.

In a mystery novel I'd once read entitled *Kingdom of Fools*, the antique dealer lured the antique-obsessed criminal into his shop with his unrivaled collection of stills. *Yes, this pot certainly looked like the still described in that book.* It made sense, but why hadn't the bootleggers hidden the evidence better? And didn't the bootleggers just sell the stuff rather than make it? My history lessons were failing me. Then I suddenly wondered if any of their descendants had known about the house. Were they after me, too?

The word *Volstead* came to mind again, but I wasn't sure why. Perhaps a quick visit to my library would reveal some answers. *My goodness. I actually have a library.* Without wasting a minute, I dashed down to the first floor. I shoved open the double doors and entered the domain of my library. I switched on every light I could find, but it did little to brighten the oppressive feel of the room's dark oak shelves and paneling.

My gaze drifted upward. With the extra light, I could now see the ceiling better, which was slightly domed and covered with a faded mural. I could make out a distant castle, dark horses, and men with swords who seemed to be caught up in a life-and-death struggle. *What a surprise in this house.* And restoring that painting would cost me a fortune. *Oh well.* Back to the matter at hand. I busied myself, searching for some reference-type books.

After fifteen minutes of going through rows and heaps of hardbound books, I finally found an old set of encyclopedias. I dragged down the correct tome, opened it, and blew off a coating of dust. Without thinking, I breathed in at the wrong time. I coughed and choked, which seemed to stir up even more dust.

Finally, after I'd calmed my hacking and my eyes had cleared, I opened the book to the letter V. With my fingers, I scanned down the page. *Va-. Ve-. Vi-.* Okay. *Vo-.* Finally. The word was actually listed there. *Volstead.* Oh, my goodness. I remember studying the Volstead Act in high school. The famous act had also been called the National Prohibition Act of 1919. But why would bootleggers give my house that name? Wouldn't it only draw more attention to the house? Or had the title come later, after they'd gone?

I eased the book shut and returned it to the shelf. *I guess you were right in your letter, Granny. There are a great many mysteries in this house. But why did you choose me to solve them?*

Later, after I'd gotten all snug on my real bed with a real mattress, I began to feel quite peculiar. The room slowly began to gyrate. I saw things on the walls that I knew had not been there before. I felt giddy and feverish and then finally dizzy. *What's happening to me? Think, Bailey.* After going to the bank, I'd eaten a late lunch with Dedra. Had I gotten food poisoning? *No, it's too late.*

Then even in my grogginess, I vaguely remembered the same symptoms happening to the heroine in a mystery entitled *The Saffron Veil*. The young woman had been given an old book from an antique store. When she handled the book, she later became delirious from a fungus that had been growing on it. The mold had worked like a hallucinogen, and the villain had then whisked the heroine away without a struggle. *But I am my own villain here. I did this to myself.* Didn't I? What should I do? Call an ambulance, or should I try to sleep it off? *God, help me.* I couldn't think straight. As I tried to get up, I fell back, groggy and ill.

The next morning, I woke up feeling a little tired but well again. I saw no funny pictures on the walls or felt any vertigo. I decided to stay away from the library until the books could be disposed of and the room renovated. But it was hard to forget that during the delirium the lines between reality and illusion had momentarily been confused, making even the dead cat and the library and the still in the attic seem like a dream. *Get a grip, Bailey. You're losing it.* I took a deep breath and let it out slowly. *Time to lighten up. You just need some good, strong coffee.*

I turned over toward the night table and saw my beta fish gawking at me. I smiled back at him. Sort of. Dedra had insisted on buying me a blue fishy in a bowl of red and white marbles. She'd christened the beta Liberty. I guess she hoped I'd talk to him. Make a friend. Mostly, though, Liberty just circled his tiny fins and made fishy facial expressions. I could tell he and I wouldn't be conversing much, but I thought he looked kind of flashy as far as fish go. He crowded into the rest of my tiny world.

Accepting the beta was indeed a positive move, though. At least this gift would keep Dedra from buying me something larger. Like a dog. A yapper at my heels wasn't what I needed. I didn't want to fool with an animal whose sole purpose in life was to tag along behind me and see what I was up to. If I'd wanted that, I could go over to Max's house and talk to him! *Oh, Bailey. For shame. That was a pretty low one, especially since he's never bothered you again.*

I stared back at the fishy. Did he expect breakfast, or did beta fish always have that hungry look? I sprinkled some flakes in the bowl and watched him gulp at his treat. Then he went back to his regularly scheduled fish poses. Not the most inspiring pet in the world.

I got up and stretched, making waking-up noises like people in normal homes. I noticed a new buoyancy in my step. I threw back the makeshift drapery and took in the day below me. Sunny, steamy, and Sunday.

This coming week, I'd make a mental note to ask Dedra about local churches. I might not be Miss Congeniality at church, but being there filled a spiritual need. I stretched my neck a bit to see down the street. No sign of Max. More good news.

At that very moment, I thought I heard a rap at the front door. Thinking it might be Dedra, I headed down the stairs, creating dust puffs with each thud. I checked the peephole and saw only an empty porch. I guess my imagination was getting the better of me again.

But that's when I heard something totally different. A fluttering sound. *Okay. Somebody can turn down the spook-o-meter now.* I thought of all those furious bats that couldn't find a way back into my attic. What about the flue? Had it been left open? Could they get in?

I heard the sound again. A frantic fluttering inside the house. Right behind me. My mind raced for answers. Droplets of sweat ran down my face. A scream would be so appropriate about now.

Just turn around, Bailey. Get it over with! I did. The fluttering came from on top of the mantle. I crept over to the fireplace, really wishing I were somewhere else. Anywhere else.

7

Deep-Dish Humble Pie

I shuddered at the bizarre sight. *This can't be happening to me again.* Some fiend had pinned a large blue butterfly to a piece of cardboard while it was still alive! It flapped frantically, jerking from the pain of being impaled. I watched the poor thing strain against the metal pin, but its writhing only brought it closer to death. *What can I do?*

With an act of will, I unpinned the butterfly from its frantic fluttering. It fell into my hand, its iridescent wings leaving behind a powdery shimmer on the cardboard. I put the winged creature to rest outside on a rose, but it no longer moved. I wanted to wash off the image from my memory, but the vivid impression seemed branded in my mind.

This can't go on. Am I now paranoid or is this demented act trying to tell me I might be the next one to die?

Whether I liked it or not, I needed to tell Dedra and maybe even Max about the incidents. No, not Max. I didn't want him to think I was a child who needed fathering.

I had to find clear thinking first. Hard without coffee, but I knew for certain the butterfly hadn't been on the mantle the previous night. Otherwise it would've been dead. It must have been placed there while I slept. Was someone still hiding in the house?

My sensitivities leaped into high gear. My mind scrambled for answers, but there were none. Dedra had a key. Max was a friend of hers, and he may have retained another copy of the key. But this was crazy thinking. Dedra and Max were both respectable people. Surely they wouldn't commit such menacing acts. My mind searched for another answer. But none came.

I have to get out of the house. Surging with fear, I ran next door and rang the doorbell repeatedly. Dedra didn't answer. I then strode over to Max's house and pounded on the door. Before I could hash through my impulsive reaction, Max's front door swung open. He raised an eyebrow and leaned against the doorway. He also grew a slow kind of grin I didn't quite approve of.

I know now my "House of Usher" had made me lose a piece of my mind, because the culmination of all nightmares came to play on Max's porch. I realized I stood barefoot and adorned in my tangerine PJs. They were modest, but I crossed my arms to cover up the words emblazed across the front that read BUSY SAWING LOGS.

"I guess you changed your mind." Max didn't fully succeed at masking his chuckle. "Need help?"

I wanted to calmly explain my predicament, but

with his cheeky attitude, I changed my mind. I raised my nose high enough to rival a pig's snout and decided to sling some blame around. "You know, ever since I said no to you the other evening, I guess you thought you could frighten me into submission."

In that instant, the front door swung open the rest of the way, revealing an undernourished blond who didn't look too welcoming. I tried to brighten my face, but I think the smile came out as straight as a window blind. "Hi," I said, wondering what sort of lion's den I'd just been thrown into.

Max cleared his throat. "Priscilla, this is my new neighbor, Bailey Walker. Bailey, this is Priscilla Nightingale. She just dropped by so we could go to church together."

Priscilla put her dainty hands on her emaciated hips and turned to face Max. "You know, this doesn't look good. A neighbor comes over in her pajamas and tells you you're trying to frighten her into submission. There's something wrong with this scene." She tapped her long fake nail against her freshly powdered cheek.

"Well, this is Mrs. Short's granddaughter. I've mentioned her to you," Max said with remarkable composure.

"I don't get it, but you know what, Max? I don't care enough to try that hard. . .you know. . .to get it." Priscilla's look heated up enough to singe hair.

Her hot gaze turned toward me for a second, and I cringed.

"And you know what else?" Priscilla said to Max in

a pouty voice. "I don't like your hamburgers on the grill. The smoke gets on my contacts. And I don't like making homemade ice cream on patriotic days. It's so '50s. And like, like, you're *so* obsessed with fixing up junk. I think you'd kill to get your hands on a beat-up old house you had your eye on. You should have known by now that I like *new* things. Pretty things—dressing up and going to galas and parties. I mean, I've never even seen you in a tux." Priscilla's mouth flew open as if she were waiting for us to gasp in horror. "In fact, the last thing I want to do is spend another minute here with you."

I cleared my throat. Did Priscilla actually say he'd kill to get a beat-up old house? I have a beat-up old house. *It's just hyperbole, Bailey. The woman is clearly losing it.*

"I'm sorry you feel that way." Max calmly crossed his arms.

"I do feel that way. I'm going. . .now. . .this very minute." Priscilla pursed her lips like a child. "Aren't you going to beg me to stay?"

"No. I don't think so," Max said.

"Okay then." Priscilla grabbed her feather-festooned purse by the door and patted Max's cheek. "It's been. . . quaint."

Priscilla stepped over the threshold with her fuchsia stilettos. I could smell her fragrance as it puffed past me. Actually, the aroma engulfed me, stinging my sinuses like noxious vapors. If there were such a thing as a cologne alarm, Priscilla would have set it off. The perfume patrol would have had to come and extinguish her. I tried not to keep going with that thought. Too much fun.

"Priscilla, don't—," Max said, "forget your keys." But instead of tossing her the ring of keys, Max walked them over to her. "Are you sure?"

Priscilla nodded her pointy little head. She said no more, which might have been considered a blessing.

"Okay," Max said. "I pray you find all the things that make you happy." Max kissed her cheek and walked back to the door.

Priscilla scuttled down the walk, her spiky heels clattering like castanets all the way. She flung her girly-girl purse into her pink convertible and never looked back.

I watched Priscilla as she sped off. *What have I done now?* I knew looking at Max would be much harder than all of my travails put together. Yes, I'd been served a slice of deep-dish humble pie.

I rubbed my neck, swallowed what felt like an elephant in my throat, and looked up at Max. His charming brown eyes weren't as sad as I'd expected. Maybe he'd fallen into denial. Or maybe he thought about having me put away somewhere. I opened my mouth first. "I am sooo sorry. I had no idea your. . .Priscilla stood just behind the door. And I'm in my nightclothes. I never, *ever* do that. I'm so embarrassed, I may never leave my house again."

"Well, that's always an option." Max grinned at me.

He raked his chunky hair back. I noticed he wore washed-out jeans that would have looked scruffy on anyone else. Max had instead created a new appreciation in me for denim pants. Striking. Was Max staring at me, or had I been caught staring at him?

"Why don't I get you a robe and some coffee, and you can tell me what's going on?" Max said.

I smelled some heavenly brew wafting out the door and wanted some badly. My need for caffeine answered for me. "Yes. Thanks. But I don't want to keep you from church."

"I think I'd better see what's wrong first. You had a real panic in your eyes when I first opened the door."

I couldn't argue with him, so I let Max escort me into his house and into what was most certainly a man's world. *Men always decorate so differently than women.* He had no bear rug on the floor in front of his fireplace, but his furniture had sharper lines and deeper colors. The rooms had no sign of knick-knack junk or a decorator's pricey urns or perfectly tossed throws. Just good, solid, well-built basics. Perhaps a reflection of the owner. "By the way, I know I shouldn't be asking you this, but. . .shouldn't you be upset? I mean about Priscilla? I just witnessed the worst breakup scene in history." *Oh brother. My mouth is just as unfastened as Priscilla's.*

"And how many breakups have you witnessed? Or should I say 'caused'?" Max winked. "I'm teasing."

I added a wince to my smile. "Mostly I've just seen breakups in movies, and those aren't real, of course. But shouldn't you be a little angry?"

"Well, I knew our dating was coming to a closure. I just didn't expect it right now. But as you know, a funny thing happened. This new neighbor lady came over and took care of everything." He grinned.

"I'm sorry. But why did you continue to date her if you felt that way? Never mind. I'm out of line for asking that." *I have no right to question his dating life. Nor should I care. Should I?*

"I don't know. Habit can be a powerful thing. Too powerful if it makes you do the wrong things."

"She wasn't your type." Those four words spewed out of my mouth like a broken water main. I should have capped it sooner. I had other business here. But as I sat on his kitchen stool watching him, my mind drifted away from my present troubles.

"I promised you a robe," Max said. "I'll go get it."

I wondered if I'd changed my mind and decided to let Max help me now—to be my big brother and watch over me like Granny Minna wanted him to. *What have I got to lose? Really? If Max became a super-pest, I could just tell him to get lost.* Of course, that could be a problem as he would never be truly lost since he only lives two doors down. But if I would agree to some restrained help, life just might get easier.

Max came back a moment later and handed me a

big brown robe. I put it on and secured the tie. It felt like a bear hug. And I caught a pleasant whiff of some manly man fragrance when my nose brushed the soft collar. *Stay focused, Bailey.*

Max poured two coffees and handed me a mug. I cradled the ceramic cup in my hands and let the steam rise to my face. I glanced around the kitchen. Granite countertops and a slate floor. *What is it with guys and rock anyway?* But I liked the look. Smart and masculine.

I watched him over the rim of my mug, wondering if I should spill the beans now about my house tribulations. "The coffee is good. Thanks."

"So, who *is* my type?" Max asked.

I couldn't believe he asked me that. "Well, you know, someone who's willing to *kill* to get a beat-up old house." *Maybe I should have kept that to myself. Oh dear.*

Max laughed. "Priscilla likes all things new, as I'm sure you gathered." He motioned for me to continue. "Please go on. Now *who* exactly is my type?"

Did he want the truth? "Perhaps someone who doesn't have to see you dressed in a tux. Or maybe someone who knows how to construct a sentence."

"Oww. That's a sharp one," Max said.

"Sorry. I'm a little out of my mind right now, so any number of bad things might come out of my mouth. Be warned."

"Tell me. . .when you first arrived, why did you say I tried to frighten you into submission?"

"Oh, that. I'm sorry. I didn't mean it. I was befuddled. Distressed. Irrational," I said, offering my most penitent expression.

"I forgive you. Now please tell me what's upset you." Max sat across from me.

I took another sip of my coffee. "When I first arrived at my house. . .just before you came over. . . there was a present for me near the stairs. When I opened the box, it contained a dead cat."

"Why didn't you tell me about it that night?" Max asked.

I dropped my gaze. "I'm sorry. It's just that I'm—"

"I know," Max said. "You're independent."

I couldn't argue with the man. But I was on a roll and wanted to continue. "Then, just now at the house, I went downstairs, thinking someone might be at the door. No one was there, but I found a butterfly in my front living room. It was one of those big, beautiful blue ones, and someone had stuck a pin through its body. . . while it was still alive." I set down my mug. "They put it on a piece of cardboard like it was a specimen. But, Max, the butterfly was still alive and in lots of pain. I realize it's just an insect, but someone went to a lot of trouble to be cruel and to have me see it suffer."

I rubbed my forehead, wondering if I had any more aspirin in my suitcase. "The butterfly wasn't there last night. That's the other part. It had to have been placed there while I slept." I pulled the robe around me even tighter as if it could take away some of the anxiety. "Who could be doing these things to me? And what do they mean?"

Max rose from his stool, frowning. "This is not good. At all. Someone is trying to scare you. But I can't imagine what neighbor would do such a thing. I mean the older couple, the Lukins, who live on the other side of you, are certainly cantankerous at times, but that's all." He stared at the floor. "But I do remember something odd a few years ago. A man wanted to buy the house from your grandmother and offered her way more than the place was worth. He never gave a reason, but he pushed hard to buy it."

"Why didn't Granny want the money?"

"She wanted to save this house for you," Max said. "Plain and simple."

"Oh."

"But that man, Buford somebody. I can't remember his last name. After he gave up on the house, he said he planned on moving to Colorado."

"But what if he didn't move?" I asked, getting a little concerned again.

"I never knew for sure. But I suppose he could be hanging around. Maybe he figures if he scares you enough, you'll put the house up for sale."

"Do you really think it could be this guy?" I asked.

"I honestly don't know. Actually, a number of people have wanted to buy this house over the years. Even the Lukins, but they didn't offer much."

Suddenly I got an itchy-type question that needed some scratching. "By the way, how much more money was that Buford character willing to pay for it?"

Max raised an eyebrow. "Forty thousand dollars more than what it was worth."

"Wow. And he didn't give you *any* reason for being so stupid or desperate?"

"Well, since it was such a large amount of money, I did ask him some questions. You know, try to needle it out of him." Max rolled up his sleeves and refilled his mug. He held up the pot. "I have plenty of coffee if you want some more."

"Maybe just a little," I said. "So, did you have any luck pressing that guy for information?"

"I'm afraid not. Buford was as personable as a brick wall." Max poured some more coffee in my mug and then sat down, gazing at me.

So, what brand of smile did Max always wear? His expression washed over me, giving me a funny rush. Nice feeling but bewildering at the same time.

"Hey, by the way, did you get your hinges fixed on that back door?" Max asked.

"I fixed the hinges myself. But I guess someone got in anyway." I picked up my mug again and let the aroma soothe me.

"I know some of this area is rundown, but all in all, it's considered a pretty safe neighborhood. So I can't imagine anyone around here doing such malicious things. Listen, when you finish your coffee, maybe we should call the police."

I shook my head.

"Why not?" Max asked.

"Long story."

Max let out a long breath. "Whoever is doing this could be dangerous. And whoever it is, is guilty of some pretty serious crimes."

"I know that. Maybe you could help me make the house more secure."

Max nodded. "I will. Maybe I could come over and check out the doors for you. You know, look for signs of a break-in. Then on Monday you could have a contractor put on new doors and heavy deadbolts. Also, if you have the money, I'd get a really good security system put in." Max took a sip from his mug.

Do I have the money? How funny. "Max. There's something else I need to tell you."

He looked up at me, waiting for me to say more.

8

A Highly Volatile Emotional State

It has to do with money." I rinsed my mug out and set it in Max's sink. *Should I really tell him about Granny's money? Can I trust him?* I turned around, and Max was suddenly nearer to me than I expected. What was that cologne? Woodsy, refreshing, and all male. They should call it "Under the Influence." Whatever it was, I wanted a bottle of it next to my pillow. I backed up a bit from Max. Now what was I going to say? "Uh, yes. I found a hole at the back of one of my closets. It's in the master bedroom upstairs where I sleep. I found three gallon jars. They were full of cash and a note from Granny."

"Mrs. Short left you *cash* in a hole in your closet?" Max shook his head. "She's still surprising me, even now."

I let out a sound almost like a giggle. I felt so comforted that Max hadn't known about the money, especially since I'd entertained the idea that he'd not only been using Granny to get to her money, but could have murdered her. *How could I think such wicked thoughts about Max?* I made the choice to trust him. "But you don't know all of it. Please don't tell anyone, but. . . well. . .Granny left me half a million dollars." It felt so good to say those words again. I had wanted to tell the whole world my good news, but I knew that could be foolish and risky. Letting Dedra know, and now Max, felt almost as satisfying as telling the whole world. I studied his expression.

"Really? That's unbelievable," Max said. "What a huge amount of money to just cram into gallon jars and just hope the right person found it."

"It is unusual. But then Granny was always a bit unconventional. And even more so toward the end of her life." I folded my arms. "And yes, before you ask, I did put the money in the bank."

"That's good. Very good." On Max's last words, he shook his finger at me. "Sorry." He put his finger away and seemed a little embarrassed. "My sisters. I guess I do that to them a little, or so they tell me."

"You lecture them?"

"I don't mean to." Max set his mug in the sink. "But I have to be careful. Older Brother syndrome."

"I'll have to keep that in mind." I wondered if he planned to treat me the same way.

A quiet came between us for a moment. "I am very grateful to Granny, you know. I really appreciate the money. I barely had enough money to buy anything."

"It is incredible news, Bailey." Max's eyes were full of warmth.

I could tell Max wanted to congratulate me a little more intimately, but he held back from a hug. Funny how a handshake would have been too little and a hug too much at this stage. Or would a hug be awkward for other reasons? But I was certainly pleased Max looked so pleased. "Thanks." All of a sudden, I felt way too hot for his bear robe. "I'm not used to the heat in Houston, although I guess you do have air conditioning. Don't you? Of course, you do." Was I making a fool of myself?

"Yes. It's pretty hot here in Houston." Max reached over me to turn off the coffeemaker. I could feel his breath on my face as he pulled back ever so leisurely. I closed my eyes. The cologne again. I was definitely under the influence. Max cleared his throat, and I jumped a little.

"I'd be interested to know how you found that hole in the closet," Max said.

I crammed my emotions back into my pocket. "Well, I remember a nightmare Granny used to talk about. All the time. In the dream, the only way out of this spooky old house was a spider-lined passage."

"But how would you have thought the dream could be connected to something real?" Max asked.

"There was a small table in the closet, and I accidentally knocked it backwards. The wall sounded funny when it hit. Sort of empty. I hammered all around that area with the heel of my shoe, and sure enough, the noise I heard sounded sort of hollow. Then I found two edges on the trim that made a square. I lifted up on the edge, and a door slid open. It was like magic."

"Your grandmother had quite a sense of humor and adventure."

"Yes, she did." I folded my arms, not really knowing what else to do with them. "So, I not only have the money to put in a topnotch security system, but the money to fix up this house."

"That's wonderful," Max said. "But I'm still curious. If that table hadn't hit the closet wall to hear the hollowness behind it, would you have ever found the opening?"

"Well, Granny did talk about her nightmare in great detail. And there were remarkable similarities. So, because of that, I think I would have noticed those openings on the trim eventually." I shrugged. "Besides, I'm a pretty snoopy person."

"Oh, really. Is that right?"

Did I see attraction on Max's face? His voice and chin lowered. Yes. I may not have dated much, but I still knew the sound of seduction. Unless it was just something gastrointestinal going on. I've noticed the older one gets, the more bodily disturbances can masquerade as romantic inclinations. I shook off my bizarre trail of thoughts.

Somewhere in all the fuss, I realized I must be in total disarray. My hair was surely tousled, but not in a sexy, windswept way. I probably had football player eyes with mascara smeared everywhere but on my eyelashes. Then worse than all of the above, I wondered what I smelled like. At least Priscilla's odor was non-organic. Oh well.

I couldn't do a thing about it this very minute anyway. "Max, I guess this means I'm sort of taking you up on the offer. Remember the contract my granny had with you? You know, the helper thing. But I'm only agreeing to it as a trial. If you become too pushy or start making too much homemade ice cream on patriotic days, I may have to fire you."

Instead of being mad at me for my teasing, Max threw his head back in a beefy laugh. And right then, I made another discovery. I liked the way Max Sumner laughed. I liked it way more than I wanted to admit. I'd best reel myself in. I felt a highly volatile emotional state coming on.

While I floated on my own hot air, Max got all professional on me. He assured me he'd be over in a few minutes to check out my house. Max walked me to the door, and I stepped out into the Houston humidity, pulling at the robe's tie.

"By the way," he said, "you were right about something." I handed his robe back to him and prepared to make a mad dash toward home. He smiled. "Priscilla really *wasn't* my type."

9

STUCK IN THE MUD PITS

Minutes later I sort of half slithered, half jigged home. For once I couldn't figure out my own emotions. They appeared as a menagerie of all human feelings, like the two drama masks plus every imaginable variation in between. In other words, I hoped I didn't have a hormone imbalance.

I had to grab the bull by the horns again, as they surely must say in Texas. But I might have come too late to my own rescue. I'd promised myself to do the life thing without becoming exposed and powerless, and within a mere forty-eight hours, I'd digressed into a vulnerable and helpless-sheep pattern. Yes. I'd become like a fluffy mammal toppling down rocky hills and getting my bumbling bum stuck in the mud pits. I could see the words plastered on my forehead: STUPID FEEBLE SHEEP.

And in addition to that, I'd already broken every one of my life rules. One: Don't get too deeply involved with people. Two: Don't share your guts. Three: Don't let people give you too much; otherwise you'll be obligated to them. Now I was beginning to wonder what was worse—breaking my life rules or making them up to begin with?

Life suddenly felt asymmetrical. The whole package. I wasn't even sure what was up or down, right or left. Would I be able to stop the person who was bent on frightening me away? Would I really be able to fix up this old place? Did I really want Max to be like a helpful brother? Miles of questions kept leading to more of the same. It felt demoralizing to think that when I hit the first real dip in my Houston life road, I'd bottomed out.

Like chasing freshly strewn marbles, I tried grabbing at bits of courage. I didn't want to be beaten— to flee in fear. I held my head high and hollered in the living room, "I am not leaving! Do you hear me?" The declaration didn't sound authoritative, but at least the sound reverberated from the walls. But why did I yell? Was I worried someone still lurked in the house? How would I ever sleep again? Apparently, someone had decided my house was one big come-and-go spook party.

But I think the person I tried to convince the most about staying was me. I could easily run. I could put my house up for sale today. I had every right to, and I knew Granny would have understood my dilemma. But in spite of everything, I felt some part of me becoming attached to this monstrosity. I cleared my throat, gritted my teeth, and made up my mind. I would stay, even if I had to sleep with one eye open.

I suddenly remembered Max had promised to head over soon, so I clothed myself properly in new jeans and a clean T-shirt. I scrubbed my face and brushed some color on my face. No doubt I smelled, so I slathered on some high-powered antiperspirant and wished I'd had time for a shower. Oh well. Max had already seen me at my worst and hadn't passed out. Then I heard a sharp rap at the door.

I opened the door to Max. The moment felt worlds apart from when he'd passed through my threshold before. He was welcome this time. "Thanks for coming."

Max frowned. "Bailey. We do need to talk about this some more. . .about you calling the police. A break-in is serious."

"Yes, it is. Please come on in." Max stepped in, and I shut the door.

"But I don't want to get a reputation early on here for crying wolf. Since we're going to make sure the house is very secure, I think it'll be okay." Even though I had no intention of calling the police, I loved the fact that Max wanted me to. *Guilty people never want to call the police, so that once again proved his innocence.*

Max put his hands on his hips, and after a weighty pause, he said, "Well, I do think some of the neighborhood kids on the other side of the bayou might have been using this place as a clubhouse. They may have had access through your broken fence in the back and then come through your back door, since it's so flimsy." He rubbed his chin. "I'm not sure, but a few weeks ago I may have seen a couple of those boys coming out of your front gate. Maybe the kids are trying to scare you off to get their clubhouse back."

"But what kind of a kid would commit these acts of cruelty?" I asked.

"I don't know. And we don't know how far they'll go. That's assuming it's the kids. I'm just making guesses here. Are you sure you don't want me to call someone?"

"I'm sure. Yes." I folded my arms like a prosecuting attorney. I wondered if my posture looked convincing or just silly.

Max went to work checking out the front door while I kept busy feeling like a helpless sheep again. "This door is starting to rot. It'll need to be replaced. If you don't mind, I want to look at the back door, too."

Max led the way through the hall into the kitchen. Apparently, he, too, along with the rest of the neighborhood, was very familiar with the layout of my house. After a quick examination, he grimaced. "This door is a joke."

"I fixed the hinges."

"But the lock is so cheap, anyone could open it with a credit card." He pointed to the offending piece of metal. "I should have warned you about that, too."

"It wouldn't have mattered," I said to make him feel better.

"Why's that?"

Did I really want to look at him while saying this?

"Because I wasn't in the mood right then to listen to anything you had to say."

"Okay. I like honesty." Max grinned at me. "As I'm sure you already know, you have another door in the library that was boarded over. I suggest you replace the two doors right now and add a reliable security system. I might be able to get crews in sometime tomorrow." Max put his hands on his hips and suddenly looked businesslike. "What do you think?"

"Absolutely. All of it. But I really want to stay with the same design on the doors. I'd like to keep as many things authentic about the house as I can. Restore it, not remake it."

"Good girl. I like the way you think."

"Well, on second thought, maybe I'll boot out the gargoyles. They never look too happy to see me."

Max chuckled.

"But." I pointed my finger in the air. "There is one *really* important alteration I must have."

"What's that?" Max asked.

"Air. I need central air right away."

"Central air is going to be expensive to install in a house like this."

"I know. But I don't care. I bought some small window units I can use for a while, but *I want central air*." I realized my voice had risen with each word.

"Yes, ma'am." Max grinned.

"Sorry."

"Well, you certainly have the money for central air now." Max headed for the kitchen counter. He opened the phone book and circled some businesses. He tapped his finger on one of the names. "These guys are the best for doors. Logan Services. They've done work for me on some houses. They're good, fair in price, and I think I can convince them to come on short notice. . . which is important here." Max flipped through the book some more and circled another name. "Mondale Security is good. Once they're finished, I can help you find somebody for central air. How does that sound?"

"It sounds perfect."

"If you want, I could call the door and security people right now and tell them it's an emergency. Which it is. And I'll bet I can get them to come tomorrow."

"I think it's hard for me to let you do this." I hoped he wouldn't question me too much.

"You mean because you don't know me very well?"

"Not just that. I. . .don't do. . .*this*." I rubbed my temples, hoping that wasn't a headache coming on.

"*This?*" Max scratched his head. "What do you mean?"

"This accepting help thing. For a long time now I've plowed through life on my own. . .kind of like a bulldozer." I suddenly realized how goofy that sounded.

"Must be lonely doing it that way all the time." Max closed the phone book. "Would it make you feel better if you could help *me* with something?"

"No."

"Are you able to tell me why?" Max asked, looking compassionate.

"I don't think so." I shoved my hair back behind my ears and jiggled the diamond drop back and forth on its chain. "I mean not right now. Maybe I'll tell you someday."

"You should take lessons from my sisters. They never hesitate for a second to have me do odd jobs for them."

"Yes, but don't you gradually resent it?" I hoped he'd give me a straight answer.

"No. Resent isn't the right word. *Exasperated* sometimes maybe when they won't change a lightbulb by themselves. But I put the kibosh to that one."

"Good for you." I smiled, hoping we could move the conversation on to safer waters.

"But your situation is different, Bailey. You have a sincere need here, and I can help. I've been remodeling homes for years now along with my realty business." Max paused and then looked directly at me. "Also, I really did want to honor the agreement I made with your grandmother."

I straightened my shoulders and put my hands on my hips. The gesture may have looked like the animals that puff themselves up to appear bigger in front of a predator. Maybe the stance made it a little less humiliating as I yielded to the domination of the male species. "Okay. I accept your help in setting up what I need tomorrow. I'll trust you to get the right guys and the right materials. *And* you can hire a company to put in a really good security system."

"Good." Max gave me the thumbs-up sign.

I shook my head and shot him a funny smirk.

"Just a suggestion: It might be wise to spend tonight somewhere else. I know you met Dedra. I'll bet she wouldn't mind if you spent the night over there."

My body sort of slumped down in the knowledge I'd have to make lots of concessions now and rely on all sorts of people to get me through this mess. I had indeed boarded a locomotive that would take me to new territory. And apparently no one in the neighborhood wanted to let me off the train. "Okay. You're right. It isn't safe here tonight."

Then Max made a few calls for me, setting up my Monday with his favorite crew and security company. He'd rescued my bumbling self up out of the mud pits. Max plopped onto one of the chairs in the sitting room. Dust rose in chugging puffs all around him, making him look like he'd just reappeared in a magic act.

"I think you may have to consider disposing of this chair," he said.

I laughed at his understatement and then suddenly noticed a cockroach cruising across the top of the high-back chair where he sat. Without warning, the brown insect flew straight onto Max's head. I screamed before I could stop myself. Then I knocked the roach off his hair, accidentally hitting Max a little harder than I'd intended. "Oh, Max. I'm so sorry. A cockroach flew on you. It was *huge*. Like a meteor landing on your head. Are you okay?"

"I'm used to the roaches." Max rubbed his head and turned to look at me. "You've got quite a vicious slap there. I'll be sure and always act like a gentleman."

I soothingly touched Max's head where I'd hit him. "I am *so* sorry I whacked you. I thought I was saving your life. Well, sort of. Does it still hurt?"

With me still standing to his side, Max reached up and gently grasped my hand. For just a moment I wanted to keep it there in his strong hand, so I did. I closed my eyes. I thought I felt the briefest brush of his lips on my fingers. And his soft breath. I felt stirrings in those seconds I had forgotten could be roused. Like an abandoned car someone had just gassed, the engine revved up soundly, surprising its driver that it could still go for a run. But thinking maybe this felt a bit awkward or inappropriate, I gently pulled my hand away from his touch.

Max seemed to come to his senses, too, as he rose up quickly and jammed his hands into his jean pockets. "Sorry. And here I said I'd be a gentleman."

"It's okay. I touched you first."

We grinned at each other. Then laughed. It felt so

good I wanted to celebrate by kissing him but didn't. I placed my hands to my side and brought my roving thoughts back into line.

Max cleared his throat. "Bailey?" he asked with a cozy look in his eye.

"Yes, Max?" I said warmly, wondering what that mouth was going to say next.

"I'm afraid roaches can get enormous here. You can choose to do one of two things. Either spray for them or invite them to dinner."

I blinked a few times, not really knowing how to respond to his sudden comedy routine on insects. I had expected sultry, not slapstick. Maybe Max had already regretted our little handholding episode.

"The same thing is true about the fire ants here. Don't ever let them get a stronghold on your house. Once they're in, they're hard to get out." Max stared at me in a funny way with his soft brown eyes. He almost said something and then seemed to catch himself. Minutes later after giving me more tips on the house and the name of a maid service that did deep cleaning, Max exited my abode to head to a late service at his church. I watched him go, wishing I'd been showered and ready to go with him.

As I'd expected of the generous-hearted Dedra, she didn't mind that I'd asked to spend the night. In fact, she was revving up to make it into an old-fashioned slumber party. Was I supposed to bring something? Like popcorn, grape soda, chocolate chip cookie dough, or maybe gummy worms?

I plunked myself down on the living room couch and watched as dust clouds billowed upward. If any angels were watching me now, I must have been a pitiful sight. I felt smelly, unorganized, and old. *Count your blessings, Bailey. At least you're no longer poor while you're busy being smelly, unorganized, and old!*

But amid my grumbling and chastisements, I kept going back in my mind to the touch from Max. Was it supposed to mean something? Or was he just a guy who got a little gushy over me slapping a roach off his head? Something felt faulty with that conclusion.

But could Max be attracted to me? I went over to the hall mirror and stared. I guess I'd looked at myself for so many years, I no longer really knew if I were a handsome woman. Did I have one of those classic faces that could go without makeup? *Get real, Bailey.* So, what really attracted Max? Why did he touch me so tenderly? Did he actually like me for me? Surely not the way I looked today.

I took another gander at myself. I'd been told I looked attractive, but I never really let it sink in. Good skin, I guess. Tight pours, no acne. Balanced facial features. Decent auburn hair when I actually let it flow down around my shoulders. Smoky gray eyes. Not startling, but decent. My neck wasn't swanlike, but it looked worth kissing. Fairly slender body. Teeth straight and white. Lips full. *Maybe I am good-looking. Don't get cocky, Bailey.*

Feeling confused and dirty, I started upstairs to shower and make a finely tuned game plan. Just then, I heard another banging noise at the door. More surprises? I guess I didn't need to lock or even close my doors in this neighborhood. Maybe I should just install a revolving door.

10

MY STRANGE LITTLE PUZZLE

I took a peek through the hole. An older African-American lady stood on my porch holding a plate of food and a warm smile. I didn't want to be obligated to anybody else, but I was starving. I opened the door. "Hi."

"Hello. I'm your neighbor, Miss Magnolia Waters. But you can just call me Magnolia." Her voice poured out like thick cream.

I became intoxicated by the smell of whatever she had on her plate. "I'm Bailey Walker. It's good to meet you."

"Well, honey, I'm so happy to meet you, too. I live across the street in that blue Victorian house."

I noticed that Magnolia had short hair peppered with gray, a huggable portly frame, and an enormous red handbag that looked as though she could use it for a weapon if necessary. I liked her style.

"I knew you wouldn't be set up for housekeeping yet, so I brought you something to eat," Magnolia said. "I have a big slice of ham here I just took out of the oven. Honey, it's hot. So you be careful. And I've got some of my homemade biscuits and good pork-laced baked beans." She chuckled like a cooing pigeon. "Folks over at Mount Zion Gospel Church say I make the *finest* desserts they've ever eaten, so I added an extra big slice of my sweet potato pie. Hope you like it. You look like you could use a little extra weight."

I hadn't smelled anything so good in all my life. I knew as soon as she released the heaping plate to me, I would consume every crumb. Maybe even lick the plate if no one was looking. Well, in my house that last part was always questionable.

"Are you going to fix up this old place?" Magnolia asked as she handed me the plate of food.

"Yes, I. . .I think I am." I stuttered on my words for some reason.

She dipped her head low. "It's got a good foundation, this house. But. . ."

"Yes?" I wondered what she was trying to say. Would it be another piece to my strange little puzzle?

"Oh, you can't listen to an old woman like me, but it's just that every time I get near this house, I just get this urge. . .to pray. I know you're going to laugh at me."

"I'm not laughing," I said.

"Yes, if I were you, I'd flatten the thing and start afresh. But don't you let me spoil this pretty day." She chuckled.

I wasn't sure what to say, so I let it go. Just then I could see an elderly couple at the end of the cul-de-sac. Were they trimming that cedar tree or were they hiding behind it?

"Who's that?" I strained my neck to see them better.

"Oh, those would be your next-door neighbors. Boris and Eva Lukin. You've seen them now, so that'll be about it until fall. They don't get out much."

"Really? Why's that?"

"They're private people. Very private. Boris and Eva are from a village in Eastern Europe. I think somebody said they came over from. . .Transylvania."

"What a lovely thought," I said.

Magnolia chuckled.

From world history class in junior college, I knew Transylvania was a real place and not just from storybooks, but I'd never known anyone in my life who'd emigrated from there. "How curious."

"They won't even open the door for me," Magnolia went on, "even when I have one of my sweet potato pies hot right out of the oven. *Mmm. Mmm. Mmm.* Just pray for 'em, honey. That's all I can say."

I thanked Magnolia for the food, and she cooed again with all my compliments. But just as she turned to leave, I betrayed my kind voice as I inquired, "Magnolia, I know this seems like an odd question, but do you like cats?" It was a new low point for me, troubling this kind woman with my doubts.

Magnolia looked shocked at my question. "Oh, honey, it is the only creature on God's good earth that I dislike. My little sister, God rest her soul, was attacked by one when she was a baby. Little Shanda died, only six months old. The animal came into her crib and sucked the very life out of her. Yes, the doctor said Shanda died of suffocation."

"Oh?" The plate nearly slipped out of my hand. "I'm so sorry." I tightened my grip.

"So, no, I don't like. . .cats." Mist filled Magnolia's eyes, and she immediately produced a hanky to wipe her eyes.

I knew then that I was more of a jerk than I'd ever imagined. How could I make this sweet woman cry like that after bringing me a plate of homemade food? "I'm so sorry I made you cry. I promise you I won't be buying any cats for pets."

"Thank you, honey. That's sweet." She shook her head. "But don't you mind me. I just get that way sometimes thinking about her. You enjoy your goodies now."

I nodded and apologized again.

Then she lumbered back down the walk, humming her own rendition of "Swing Low, Sweet Chariot" as her red purse wagged behind her.

Nestled inside the plastic wrap, I noticed Magnolia had included throwaway utensils. Perfect. I wasn't looking forward to eating her baked beans with my fingers. Magnolia had thought of everything. I shook my head. I'd never be able to pay back all these neighbors for their help. *But then, Bailey, maybe they don't want anything from you. Just that "joy of giving" thing.* Well, those certainly weren't thoughts that rattled in my brain very often.

I eased down on the couch, careful not to rouse the dust bunnies, and began to gobble up my feast. I sighed at the taste of real food, the thoughtfulness of someone who didn't even know me, and the mysterious ways of God.

Yet even as my heart swelled with gratefulness, I felt anxious, too. Magnolia had said that little Shanda had died of suffocation. She'd blamed their cat. Could Magnolia feel a sense of retribution? Never. Yet snippets of things kept hanging in the air, making everyone seem guilty and yet no one at all. Maybe I'm still under the influence of that hallucinogenic fungus!

The same facts remained. Someone was trying to scare me. Possibly for some kind of sick pleasure or to remove me from the house. But why? Granny promised no one knew about the jars of cash. Not even Lakes. So what was so enticing about a house in ruins?

I finished my meal and double-checked to make sure the house was empty. All clear. After showering, I slid into some tan capris and a white knit shirt. Then I packed up my most important belongings and headed next door for a little "slumber party." Dedra had become so keyed up about the evening she wanted us to get an early start.

I reached for the doorbell, but the door suddenly burst open. "Hi." I picked up my suitcase. "I really appreciate what—"

Dedra, decked out in tie-dyed overalls, rushed out to hug me, nearly cutting off my air. "I'm so glad you're here."

"Me, too." Once I hit the inside entry of her house, my whole body relaxed. "Oh, air conditioning. That *does* feel good." The truth was I'd excreted enough salty sweat in my house recently to cure a truckload of hams. *I must be fitting in here a bit. Even my thoughts have that Texas twang now.*

Dedra clapped her hands. "This will be so much fun. But I am sorry about all that horrible mischief. Max told me. We need to talk. Have you called the police yet?"

I shook my head. "No. Tomorrow we're creating a fortress next door."

She took my suitcase and headed into the bowels of her house. I followed. An array of oil and watercolor paintings adorned the walls. I wondered if she were a painter.

"In case you're wondering," Dedra said. "I'm an artist, and I work out of my studio here at home."

I paused in the hallway to look at one of her paintings, a creepy Gothic mansion surrounded by dead cedar trees. The house looked exactly like mine. "This painting. It looks like Volstead Manor."

"It isn't, though." Dedra said quickly. She reached down to pick up an envelope from a small table. She retrieved a rather ornate letter opener from a drawer and ever so slowly slid the blade along the top of the envelope. "It's just a house I wanted to paint. Well, one I had to paint."

What in the world did that mean? A kind of nosiness welled up inside me, along with the slightest panic. "I'm curious. Where did you get the idea for the house then?" *Oh dear. Did that come off confrontational?*

Without looking at the contents, Dedra slipped the envelope into her pocket and left the letter opener on the table. "The painting came from a dream I had. I woke up in the night in a cold, cold sweat. I couldn't shake the dark vision I'd seen. So I rose, around midnight I think, and started to paint the house I'd seen in my sleep. I had that dream exactly one year before the night of your arrival. Do you think that's unsettling?"

All righty then. Boy, this conversation had certainly taken a creepy turn. "No. I think it's just a coincidence. And you were dreaming about what you were used to seeing. You live in a neighborhood full of very old houses. It's natural that your unconscious life would dip into your conscious life for images. And with my house being next door—"

"Like I said, it's *not* your house." Dedra's left eye seemed to get a sudden spasm. She pushed on her eyelid.

Oh dear. I've muffed this one. Come on, Bailey. Think of something sincere and positive. "By the way, your work is quite good."

"Thank you. I'm hoping you'll buy a few after you get your house repaired. Especially since you're so rich now."

Dedra winked and suddenly donned the same sunny expression I'd grown to think of as "hers." I sighed inwardly, glad the conversation had moved on.

"Well, are you ready for our big night?" She held out her arms as if she were offering me prizes on a game show.

I nodded, perhaps too swiftly, trying to show some enthusiasm.

"By the way, what kind of security system are you getting?" Dedra asked.

I shrugged. "I'm not sure yet."

"Well, I'll be going on some trips for my art shows, so I'll give you my key and security code. I know you'll want to do the same."

"I. . .uhh." *What should I say?*

"I mean, that's what friends do. Right?"

I nodded, wondering why she seemed so insistent about exchanging keys and security codes. Was she upset because she was about to lose access to my house? But if Dedra helped me tuck my cash safely away at the bank, then what would she be after? Or was it just a control thing? Maybe she felt that the mark of a trusting friendship was to trade house keys. Since I hadn't dealt with friends in so long, I hardly knew what was expected. But the moment felt awkward. The way I saw it, I had two choices. I could let Dedra's painting episode and her comments keep me bug-eyed all night, or I could let it go and enjoy the evening. I chose the second option. *What is that odd smell?* Reminded me of burnt popcorn.

Dedra shepherded me into a den with a big screen TV. "I've made us some buttery popcorn, and I have all kinds of sodas. My favorite is grape, but you'll have to tell me what you like. I have a couple of alien movies for us to choose from. And we can make a batch of cookies later if you want or do some face painting. I know it all sounds silly, but sometimes lady-friends have to be silly. Don't we? It helps us bond and de-stress. Don't you think?"

"Sure." I hoped it wouldn't be a long night.

"Please sit down. I think you'll like that sofa."

Her lavender marshmallow-like couch swallowed me up whole. The room looked cool and feminine with pastels sort of ruling the space. Dedra's dwelling appeared more traditional than Bohemian. I wondered what I'd expected. Beads hanging in the doorways and red scarves over the lampshades?

After we'd chatted for a while, Dedra suddenly rose from her cross-legged position and threw a pillow at me. Stacks of fluffy pillows sat all over the living room, but I had no idea she really intended to use them. I grabbed one up from her arsenal and threw it at her head-on, making quite a good shot. Then a pillow war broke out like none other. I won, of course, making the most continuous hits.

Later, after our alien movie had scared us silly, we made a double batch of chocolate chip cookies and ate a scandalous amount of raw dough. All the uncomfortable moments I'd felt so keenly at my arrival had somehow dissipated. We'd even gotten into a goofy mode and laughed until we couldn't breathe. Of course, that was always the bonding stage. I just hoped the connection could last, since I was beginning to welcome friendship feelings back that had long since gone dormant. Yes, in spite of our bumpy start, Dedra's slumber party had been a success. But Monday soon rose with the sun, and it was time to head home.

Twenty-four hours later, after my house had been redone to rival the security of Fort Knox, I finally relaxed. Over the next few weeks, I had no other terrorizing incidents. The game, whatever it had been, appeared to be over. In fact, minus the repair guys, all became quiet. Well, at least as quiet as a neighborhood could be with Dedra next door.

The house started coming together. Of course, it helped to have sufficient cash to pull it off. The crews cleaned all the first- and second-story rooms, making them sparkle. The wooden floors and oak wainscoting came to life with oil soap and polish. Now it would be easier to see what repairs were needed.

During that time, I stocked the kitchen shelves and the fridge with food, discarded some of the old furniture, had wooden blinds installed throughout the house, bought appliances, and started the estimates for the repairs and central air. I hired a highly recommended landscaper by the name of Wilbur Murdock. He redid the front yard in all kinds of pretty foliage. Caladiums, yaupon holly, Mexican feather grass, and a myriad of flowers now festooned the front of the house and walkway. Except for some outdoor lighting, I decided to leave the backyard more primitive-looking for now.

I had more window units put in temporarily, until I could have my permanent solution built in. I'd leave the drapes, rugs, wallpapering, painting, bathroom renovations, and furniture buying to work on more gradually. Those decisions would take lots of planning and time. In the meantime, I purchased some card tables and folding metal chairs to use while I cooked up a long-term plan.

Watching the house come together was much more of a thrill than I'd ever expected. The crews Max recommended had been great, and I'd worked so hard I started to see muscles emerging on my arms. I even let Max help out, because he loved the process, too. In fact, I wondered what kind of a letdown I'd feel when it was all over and the house was a masterpiece again. All the sweat and fun would be over. But for now, contentment began to rule my life.

Amid my collective pleasure, I'd let Dedra talk me into a series of blind dates with supposedly gorgeous Christian men from her church, which was now my church as well. I must have said yes to the dates when I'd let down my guard. But I knew Dedra meant well. She was just trying to keep me from joining the Old Maids' Club, which did indeed have a lonely ring to it.

But over the weeks, my thoughts kept drifting back to Max. Our relationship had evolved into what Granny had set up, so that spark we'd experienced before between us had apparently faded into nothing. Part of our new arrangement felt good, but on other occasions, our brother/sister thing felt as natural as if we were trying to coax an armadillo into a prairie dog hole.

Oh brother. Where did that come from?

But I had turned some kind of corner and wanted to be thankful for the sweet smell of roses as I tried to forget the prickly parts. Thinking of Max in a romantic way seemed to be one of those thorns to be avoided. And really, I'd never had a brother or sister before. Since the terror had ceased, I no longer entertained suspicions about Max, Dedra, or Magnolia, and the idea of having them for family started to grow on me. And, I guess because of them, I'd broken all my life rules. Laws that needed a little breaking.

And now because of my newer life, I waited for the doorbell to ring and to announce my first blind date.

I was to go out with a guy named Dorian Grayer. I wondered if he'd be some ancient coot with tight skin. *Oh well.* The Dedra Dating Game would soon be over, and I could move on to my own manhunt. But the word manhunt made me cringe. Marriage was not a totally appalling idea, but I guess I'd always thought love would come more naturally.

I hadn't dated much over the years. Mostly other Realtors who just wanted to talk about their listings, and a few guys from my church with whom I'd had nothing in common except for loving Jesus. Could I have it all like my parents? A romantic zap as well as common spiritual and earthly goals? What a package that would be. Put him on the auction table. I'd line up to make a bid. In quiet moments, when I'd had too much time to reflect, I thought maybe that man already existed and lived two doors down.

As I sat waiting for my blind date, I dug back into a mystery I'd been reading entitled *The Bush Master.* The novel seemed to be about a murderer whose strategy was to frighten the victims bit by bit and then hide and watch the struggle from a distance. Like a snake hiding in the bushes. Then when his victims' fears had faded and he'd tired of the game, he would strike without mercy. *Okay, maybe on second thought, I don't really like where this plot is going.* I closed the book, wondering if all my suspicions were so dulled that I could no longer recognize peril even if it were close enough to strike at me.

Bing. Bong.

I jumped. Guess I still wasn't used to having a doorbell. But it certainly sounded better than all the pounding and knuckle rapping. I guess it was my date, Dorian, waiting at the door with my Cinderella slipper. I rolled my eyes.

I walked to the door in a blue silk skirt and blouse, pearl earrings, and high heels. I had at least prepared for a lovely evening. I opened the door, stood gaping, and mumbled, "Hi, there." Did that really come out of my mouth, or was it only raspy air?

Dorian certainly wasn't an old coot with tight skin. He stood tall, tanned, and with more Greek angles than the Parthenon. He must surely belong on a billboard somewhere. Or maybe spread across a men's cologne ad in a magazine. Was he talking to me? "Oh. Please come in. Dorian Grayer, right?"

"Yes," he crooned, placing his hand over his heart. "That's *moi.*"

And so I spent the evening with Mr. Apollo, but somewhere during the three hours and sixteen minutes, the Greek profile began to look more like Dudley Do-Right. In fact, I learned enough about Dorian to write his blurb in a dating service brochure. He loved fast cars, expensive clothes, and all things Greek. *What a surprise.* He hated tuna salad and intimate talks, and he still lived at home with his aunt Polly and his uncle Buford. Hmm. Could it be the same Buford that schemed to buy my house? *Nah.*

Well, at least the evening hadn't been a total loss. The food at Sterling House had been superb. So later, back on my porch in the clammy heat, I waved my final good-bye to Dorian. Then I became consumed with the need to flick my pinching shoes across the room and peel off my hosiery, which were now melting onto my legs.

As I pulled my keys out of my evening bag, I noticed someone walking on the sidewalk toward my house. A man. In the dim lamplight. Did I know him? I fumbled with my ring of keys to find the house key. Just when I found the right one, the keys fell on the porch, making a clinking sound. I wondered if the game was up, as in *The Bush Master*, and the murderer had come out of the bushes to strike me down.

I looked again. The shadowy figure moved toward me at a faster pace.

11

TEN CATS THROWN INTO A DOGHOUSE

I scrambled for my keys on the porch. Should I scream for help? I heard the man yell something. *What did he say?*

"Bailey. It's me. Max."

I slowed my wild heart. *What a relief. I'm not going to die after all.* "Max? Really? I thought you were an ax murderer coming to cut me to pieces."

Max laughed. "I guess you couldn't see me. I'm sorry I scared you." Max strode through the open gate with a confident stride. He looked me over. "Wow. You look so. . .delectable."

"Thanks." How startling, coming from Max. The way he said *delectable* made me do a shivering thing inside, which I had to admit, wasn't unpleasant. And he wasn't bad-looking himself in his white shorts and sports shirt. He also possessed a five-o'clock shadow that forced one of my eyebrows to arch against my will. He didn't seem to have a clue how handsome he looked. I just cleared my throat and decided to keep my thoughts to myself. "I was at Sterling House tonight." I twirled my skirt like a flirty junior higher. *Bailey, what a silly gesture.*

"Yeah. I knew you went there," Max said.

I suddenly wondered if news traveled faster around here than it happened. "Well, how did you know? Are you keeping track of me?" I felt a little teasing was in order.

"No. Dedra mentioned it to me. Whether I wanted to know or not." Max walked a couple of steps closer to me.

"Oh. And *did* you want to know?"

"Yes. No." He frowned. "It didn't really matter."

It was the first time I'd seen Max truly flustered, and I delighted in the way the lines etched around his eyes as though he didn't know quite what to say. I reveled. I gloated. Did my face look too smug?

"So, how *was* your date with. . .Dorian?" Max finally asked.

"The evening was. . .in a class by itself," I replied. "So, is this why you came over? To inquire about my date?" I tried to keep my smile below the surface.

"No. Not really. I wondered if there'd been anymore incidents at your house."

"None, I'm happy to say."

"Good," Max said. "And I wanted to give you this new list of contractors you'd asked for. You know, for when you remodel the bathrooms. I think any of these guys will give you a fair shake." Max handed me the list, and for a second, our hands touched.

"Thanks." I stuffed the list in my purse, feeling a

little disappointed. A pesky mosquito droned around my head. I swatted at it. Max stepped back. Recalling the roach episode, he must have thought I was going to really let him have it.

He turned to go back down the walk. "Well. good night."

"Good night." When Max reached the gate, I felt a sudden need to stop him. But another familiar tug came along with it. *Don't get involved. Don't call out his name. Nothing long-term can come of it, Bailey, girl.* I ignored my warnings. "Max?"

He turned back to me. "Yes?"

The air seemed heavy with something—humidity, yes, but a little more. Expectancy? "Would you like to come in for a cup of coffee? It's the good stuff. But you'll have to sit on a miserably hard folding chair."

"Got decaf?" Max asked.

"Yes." Expectancy now became eagerness.

As I tooled around in the kitchen making us some coffee and heating up a few pumpkin muffins, I noticed he never left my side. He seemed to enjoy puttering around with me. But at one point Max cornered me in the curve of the kitchen counter. I wondered if my breath was fresh. "Do you need something?" I asked with the slightest quiver in my voice.

Max chuckled.

I hadn't heard him laugh that way before. A low one with "connotations." Nice.

"I was reaching for two spoons," Max said. "Aren't they in the drawer behind you?"

Good grief, Bailey. Get ahold of yourself. He was just reaching for something to stir his coffee with! "Yes, the spoons. Of course. Let me get you one."

"No problem. I'm getting to know my way around. I did help repair these cabinets. Remember?"

"I do. . .remember." So much for those high-powered air conditioners. I was now sweating like ten cats thrown into a doghouse. We sat on folding chairs around my little card table. Max didn't seem to mind. As he sipped his coffee, I cradled my head in my hand. I tried not to stare, but I wanted a good look at him. I saw the highlights in his hair from being out in the sun and the muscles on his arms. He looked at me suddenly, and I hoped I hadn't been drooling. I looked down at my coffee and took a long swig. The aroma felt soothing like a comfy blanket. "You were right about the bats. But I got rid of them."

"How did you do it?"

"Stuffed my pillow into the broken window while they were out on the town."

Max laughed. "Why not? If it works." He took a bite of his muffin. "These are good. Buttery and warm. Just the way I like them."

"Thanks." I licked my lips.

"But I haven't been back up there. It's kind of creepy."

"Creepy?" Max said. "As spunky as you are?"

"Spunky?" A melodious laugh gurgled out of my mouth. What a sound. "Would you mind taking a look with me before you go? You know, to make sure they didn't come back."

"Oh, so this coffee thing was really a ploy to get me to check out your bats."

"No. Not at all. I wanted to, you know. . .to thank you for all your help these past weeks. You've been so. . .you know. . .accommodating. And coffee is the universally accepted form of thank you. Well, *and* cash. And Granny took care of that." *What just came out of my mouth? Was I still subconsciously troubled about their silly contract?* "Sorry. What I'm trying to say is—"

"Don't worry about it. I know what you're trying to say. Listen, before I go, I don't mind having a look up there."

The lovely moment was over. I had butchered it beyond recognition. But then, was I trying to create something here? Maybe smothering the mood wasn't a bad thing, considering the alternative.

After we finished our snack, I put on something more appropriate for our attic adventure. We then stomped up the stairs to the third floor, making hollow pounding noises all the way. I sniffed the molasses-thick air. Would I ever be able to get rid of that musty smell around here, or was it a permanent fixture like the gables? I switched on the upper light, and we stepped onto the third floor.

"Along the edge over there are the soft boards." Max pointed to the west side. Without hesitation, he then strode to the attic door and opened it. He flipped on the inner light and peeked in. "Okay so far."

We both crept in and took in the rather comical sight—my pillow with the chubby cupid pillowcase was still wedged securely in the window.

"The bats are probably feeding right now, but it looks like your idea worked," Max said. "Be sure and add that window to your repair list."

"I did."

"Good." Max pointed to the tower. "Do you mind if I look inside while we're up here?"

"Please do."

I opened the small door, and then we stepped into the tower. As we sat down on the wooden benches that lined the outer walls, we could see some of the sparkly lights of the neighborhood from up there. Tops of some trees. The moon. *It's called a setting for romantic inclinations, Bailey.* "It's nice up here. This niche might make a great place for reading mysteries. Don't you think?"

Max seemed to be a million miles away. Probably still remembering Priscilla and thinking how I'd run her off. And how he missed her. And how I'd ruined his life. *Nah.*

Silence ruled the room for a few moments. They weren't uncomfortable minutes, just quiet. Max cleared his throat. "Bailey?"

"Yes?"

"I need to ask you something."

"Okay." I truly wondered what he had on his mind.

Max stood up and stepped closer to me. Suddenly I heard a loud crack. The boards underneath him gave way like a trapdoor, sending Max down through the floor.

I screamed. "No!"

Dust flew up all around me. I dropped to my knees and looked downward. I could see Max hanging on to a joist, but he was about to drop down into a second-story bedroom. "Grab my hand. I can pull you up!"

I wiped the damp hair out of my eyes. *Bailey, you can do this.*

"Okay."

"Be careful. It's too far to fall without breaking something." I coughed, trying to clear all the dust from my throat.

Max released one hand and grabbed mine in a solid grip. There was no way I was going to let go of him now.

"Bailey?" Max asked.

"Yes?" What was wrong?

"Will you go out with me?" the now-familiar voice asked from the deep.

12

A Matchmaker Gone Awry

What?" I almost let go of his hand from the shock.
Did I hear him right? I thought he was supposed
to be struggling for his life.

"A date. I'm *asking* if you'll go out with me."

"Right this minute? This is crazy." I still clung to
his very warm hand and arm.

"I want an answer," Max said.

"I thought you said you were going to be like a
brother to me."

"I don't need another sister. I have plenty. I don't
see you that way, Bailey."

"Then my answer is yes." I yanked on his hand and
arm with renewed gusto.

Max got enough leverage to brace his arm on the
floor and then lift himself up out of the hole. Boards
he'd just used to hoist himself up on fell, making a
crashing echo. He glanced downward and moved away
from the opening. "I was about to drop, waiting for
your yes," he said grinning.

How can he joke at a time like this?

Max dusted off his shorts and shirt, but the effort
was useless. He had become the color of dirt. "Guess

it's a good thing I do all those pushups."

I was so relieved he'd come out alive I wanted to hug him. But something held me back. "You really scared me. I'm so sorry about the floor. Are you all right?"

Max nodded as he focused on my lips.

His hair appeared all ruffled and dusty, but he looked very well indeed. I looked up at him and felt a flush take over my body. His soft brown eyes looked intense. "Hey."

"Hey, yourself." My mouth was about to betray me. "Okay, if I'm not a sister-type to you, then how do you see me?"

Yeah. I saw it for sure. That smoldering thing men do right before they kiss a woman. My face must have given him the thumbs-up, because Max instantly made the distance between us disappear. He scooped me into an embrace.

I threw my arms around his neck and finished reeling him down to my mouth. I shocked myself, not even caring if I, too, became the color of dirt. What fired up between us had no brotherly-sisterly feel to it. It was as if someone had thrown gasoline on a pilot light. As we moved to more serious ground, a warning bell went off in my head. If we kept up this pace, we'd be toast.

I pulled back. *Good grief, Bailey, for somebody who's afraid to open her heart, you sure have no problem opening your arms!*

Max took in a deep breath, obviously trying to calm his breathing. "You kind of surprised me."

I moistened my lips. "I surprised myself. Believe me. Sorry. I think I *embarrassed* myself, too. We haven't even been on a date yet." Boy. None of my dates back home had ever made me feel that way. Was I making up for lost time, or was there something else going on? Something that fixed the short circuit to my heart. I had already known the latter rang true. I just didn't know what I should do about it.

"Well, if we count all those times I came over to work on your house as a date, this is our fourteenth."

"You thought of those workdays over here. . .as dates?" I asked.

Max took me into his arms again. "Yes and no. I wanted to help you. I enjoyed being with you. *And* I've wanted to kiss you since the night you moved in."

"Really?"

"Yeah. But I think you would have kicked me out."

"Yes, I would have." I loosened myself from his cozy embrace.

Max looked me over. "I think I got you kind of grimy."

"Well, it's my floor you fell through, so I feel I'm the one who got you dirty."

Max frowned and cupped my cheek as if it were delicate crystal. "I think I scratched you with my whiskers. Your face looks a little pink."

"I'm blushing." I grinned, still self-conscious. "So, I guess we're going out."

"Yes, we are," Max said. "Hopefully by then I'll have recovered from that kiss."

"So was it worth falling through the floor?" I glanced away from his gaze.

"Definitely. While I was down there, I realized I didn't want to see my Maker before asking you out. Or before kissing you."

"Well, I'm glad my dangerous floors are good for something."

"By the way, I think you'd better add this hole to your repair list," Max said in a paternal tone.

I looked directly at him and saluted. "Yes, sir."

Max caught my fingers in his hand. The moment heated up again. Warm. Sweet. Inviting.

We reached for each other, and then we both stopped before melting again. Max said, "We have something. . .good going on here. Like a gift. I don't want to spoil it. I think I could. I'm very attracted to you. But there's more here. And I want us to have time to explore. . .what it is." As soft as a petal brushing against my skin, Max kissed my hand. I closed my eyes to absorb the sweet pleasure of the gesture.

When he finished, I opened my eyes.

Max smiled and let go of my hand. "How about dinner tomorrow night?"

"Yes. Oh no. I've got a date. I'm sorry, Max."

"With whom? If you don't mind my asking?"

"Someone Dedra set me up with. Another blind date, I'm afraid." Wow. That disclosure certainly spoiled the moment. "Some guy named Rupert Rutledge. Is Rupert a real name?" I said to diffuse the damage.

"That guy? I know him. We all go to the same church. Faith Community."

"That's the church I started going to recently."

"Really?" Max said. "I haven't seen you."

"It's a very big church."

Max sat down on a bench and looked up at me. "Rupert's okay, I guess. Stinking rich with an emphasis on *stinking*. Some women in our singles' group would kill to go out with him."

"Then what's he doing going out with me on a blind date?"

"I don't know. Maybe he's having a slow week." Max grinned.

I wanted to push him back into the hole. "What a thing to say."

"I'm teasing," Max said. "Okay. He's not a bad guy. It's just. . .well. . .I think it's obvious now why I'd rather it be me and not Rupert." He pointed a finger in the air. "Oh, and just for your safety, I think you'd better take your umbrella with you on your date with Rupert."

"Why?"

"He's quite a spitter when he gets to talking."

I laughed and sat down across from Max. Just as

I was about to keep the banter going, I saw a flash of light from the Lukins's upper window again. Just like the night when I'd arrived. And I could see the faintest shadow of a figure running across my backyard. How odd. Then the ghostlike figure, no more than the size of a boy, disappeared beyond the fence. I held my expression steady, not wanting concern to flicker across my face. No sense in ruining the evening with speculation.

But could Max have been right? A gang of boys wanted their clubhouse back, which just happened to be my home? Tonight. Alone. I was determined to find out. I decided not to invite Max along even though I knew he'd want to be included in my investigations. While he was obviously not the criminal of my first wild imaginings, I still held back. Why? I wasn't totally sure. *Oh, dear, what is Max saying?* I decided to drop in where we'd left off. "Well, you could always ask me out for another time."

"I will," Max said. "How about Sunday lunch after church?"

I dropped my gaze. "I'm sorry, Max. Dedra's been at it again."

"You have *three* blind dates in a row?"

"I don't usually do this blind-date thing. But Dedra thought she was helping me. Actually, I set it up this way just to get them over with. I don't really want to go. But I made a promise." I tried looking defenseless, but I don't think he was convinced.

"Dedra is a great gal, but don't let her do this to you. She's a bit of a matchmaker gone awry."

"And what if she decided to set me up with you?' I asked.

"Then I would say she had excellent taste, and I would highly recommend her suggestion."

I laughed, wishing I didn't have *any* blind dates. But Max suddenly looked quite serious. "Is something wrong?"

"You know, Dedra is a caring and generous person."

"Yes, she is." I wondered what was on Max's mind.

"Because you are a friend of hers now, I want you to know she's had some struggles. Several years ago, she voluntarily entered a psychiatric ward at one of the hospitals here. While she was getting treatment for bipolar disorder, she later told me she'd struck one of the doctors. It frightened her, and since she has no family, she's asked some of the neighbors to watch out for her. She has some difficulty when she's off her pills."

"I'm so sorry Dedra has suffered like that. I can't imagine." Max seemed to study my expression.

"I'm telling you this, so as a new friend to her, you can help us watch for the signs. . .that she's not taking her medication."

"What are the signs?" I asked, still trying to let the news sink in. Dedra appeared so "together" all the time—except for those rather peculiar moments when I'd first arrived at our slumber party.

"She can get super keyed up or so down she can barely function. I think lately she's been faithful about her medicine. The incident in the hospital really scared her."

"I will. . .watch out for her, too." After a long pause, I touched Max's arm. He'd obviously been a good friend to Dedra.

Max fell silent for a moment and then squeezed my hand. "So, what guy did you get stuck with for lunch on Sunday?"

"Lee Yorker," I said like someone who'd been chewing on a lemon.

Max groaned.

"So is Lee a really loaded spitter, too?" I asked.

Max tugged on my sleeve while he stared at me. "No. He has his own unique failings."

I laughed. "You know, I accepted the dates because I didn't really know there was anything between us. Well, that's not totally true. I knew. I felt. . .things. But I just didn't know. . .you know, what we. . .I'm digging a deep hole here, aren't I? Can you help me out. . .please?"

"I don't think so." Max leaned back against the window frame. "I'm enjoying this."

I cocked my head at him.

"Look. I'm not asking you to cancel your dates. I'm simply hoping they'll be unforgettable disasters."

"Like I said, unless you've given up on me already,

you might try asking me out for another time."

"I'm almost afraid to ask. Okay. How about tomorrow at noon? That should still give you plenty of time to get all gussied up for your big evening date." Max winked.

Or was that a twitch in his eye? "It's a deal." I stuck out my hand for a shake. "Where are you taking me?"

"It's a surprise." Max kissed my hand again. This time even more slowly.

"I think you'd better go," I said softly, "before we *both* do something we'll regret."

Max honored my suggestion and said good night. He headed down my walkway whistling "Three Blind Mice." I chuckled, thinking about the promise of our date. He'd said the destination was a surprise. I'd never been big on surprises, but I had to admit I was really looking forward to spending some time with Max. I sniffed the palm of my hand. *Mmm.* Max's cologne still lingered on my skin. Nice.

Now, for a bit of snooping. No sense in telling Max. He'd only worry about me. I took my trusty flashlight and headed out the back door. I walked maybe one hundred feet to the back fence. I shined the light along the edge until I saw a section of the fence that was not only broken, but had an opening at the bottom. I got on my knees for an up-close look. The gap was certainly big enough for a kid to crawl through, and the dirt on the bottom had been worn hard and smooth as if someone had been scooting through the spot. Often.

I angled the beam back and forth but saw nothing more. I dusted myself off and then noticed a small black apparatus sitting next to a rock. On closer inspection, the gadget appeared to be a two-way radio. A light on the front blinked green. Someone had left it turned on. Whoever it was must have been in a hurry. Since I'd found it resting on its side, the person appeared to have dropped it by accident.

I headed back to the house with my morsel of evidence. I felt somehow this was my first real clue to the events that were intended to drive me from my home. In fact, was I being watched right now? Had someone wanted to draw me out? Here I was, silly enough to be alone in the dark. I heard the lonely hoot of an owl and a sudden rustling just beyond the fence. It was enough to send me racing toward the house. I slammed the door shut, triple locked it, turned on the security system, and let my body sink to the floor. The light on the walkie-talkie flickered off. The batteries must have just run out.

I fumbled through my newly assigned junk drawer and found some AA batteries to replace the old ones. The green light blinked at me again.

Dog-tired, I quickly readied myself for bed and placed the two-way radio on my night table next to my beta fish, Liberty. He looked at the device with curiosity and then went right back to looking bored.

Later, in bed, my thoughts grappled with the new bits of information. The two-way radio. Was it a sign or just a kid playing with a toy? And what sad news about Dedra. I would always help her if she wanted me to, and I would certainly pray for her. But in spite of my good intentions and prayerful concern, I couldn't help but wonder what other acts of aggression Dedra was capable of. *No, way, Bailey. What are you thinking? Maybe I'm getting so paranoid I'll be the one in need of a psych ward.*

Then my thoughts unwound and floated over to Max. He certainly seemed like a great Christian guy. Funny. Sweet. Confident. We had the same interests. There could be no doubt I sensed some kind of sparkle between us that went beyond attraction. Yes. The word *risk* had come back into my life. It seemed unavoidable. But now I was speeding headlong into an abyss where all was unknown and everything was up for grabs. Including my heart. I wondered if it could stay in one piece this time. Some part of me still doubted that love could triumph over all.

Then I thought of Max's mouth on mine and the electric kind of squeeze he gave me. A tingle flowed over me just as it had before. Wow. What a rush. But I'd need to put all those thoughts out of my head or I'd never get any sleep.

As I burrowed down into the softness of my new bed, I could sense the sandman approaching.

Out of my floating bliss, I heard a sound. The tiniest scratching noise. I opened one eye and gaped at the two-way radio. The green light not only blinked, but I could hear the faintest voice emerging. A woman's angry voice. I wiped away my bleariness, grabbed the radio, and placed it firmly against my ear. "The plan is not working," I heard a woman say. "Seth, we'll need to. . ." And then I heard only white noise. I slapped the radio, but I heard nothing else. Perhaps it had landed on a rock earlier and was damaged.

I played the woman's words over and over in my head. "The plan is not working. Seth, we'll need to. . ." Who was talking? Had I heard that voice before? What plan wasn't working? Was there indeed a plan to flush me out? And how many people were involved? And who in the world was Seth? *Seth is a guy's name, popular perhaps a decade ago.*

Hmm. Oh well, moving on. I assumed the two-way radios only had a short radius, so that meant they couldn't be too far away. But why not use cell phones? And still, I couldn't imagine what anyone would want from such an old house like mine. My thoughts went back to the gallon jars of money again, but I felt certain Granny had told no one about the cash. And as far as any guilty kids, the woman certainly wasn't part of a gang wanting their clubhouse back.

After hours of tedious deciphering that led nowhere, I succumbed to the sandman and drifted off into some serious slumber.

I woke early the next morning to greet my hired crews and they set to work with a variety of bangs and clatters. I glanced over at the two-way radio and chuckled. Now in the clear light of day, the voice I'd heard seemed more like a misinterpretation than evidence. I felt foolish for even taking the gibberish seriously. I said good morning to Liberty and slipped out of bed.

Max had told me to dress "nice casual" for the day, so I picked out a short white jean skirt and a frilly light purple, scoop-necked blouse. The need for the frothy female look had always eluded me, but sometimes a woman had to do something out of her fashion comfort zone. And this was that day.

Like fine car wax, the moisturizer that I slathered on my face gave it a nice glow. Then I applied everything else in my makeup case to give my face an overall showroom finish. I stared at my reflection and decided to bring out the big guns. Or should I say, "turbo engines"? I revved up the curling iron and my superhold hair lacquer. When all was creamed and preened, I thought I looked like a pretty decent display model. Perhaps a little yellow convertible coupe. Too bad Max wasn't a car dealer. I chuckled at my little joke. *Is Bailey in a good mood, or what?*

I grinned, wondering what had happened to me and what sort of mind-bending fairy dust had been sprayed on me to make me so intense about my appearance and so goofy in the head. Those ethereal creatures must have skipped the sprinkling and decided to drop a cargo load on me with a crop-dusting plane. In short, I'd become a hopeless emotional pixie.

Fingering Granny's necklace, I wondered if she'd be happy about Max asking me out, or had she only thought of him as a brother-helper type for me? But this date today was really only an assessment, not a commitment. It represented a test to see what hid behind all the emotions that had surfaced between us.

I fidgeted for the last time in front of the bathroom mirror. Did I hear the doorbell? I looked at my watch. Right on time. I headed downstairs and swung the door open. I looked at Max's smiling face and decided not to cloud up the day with the worries of the previous night.

Max stood there in his khakis and periwinkle blue shirt. Handsome. His eyes got kind of big, so I thought maybe he appreciated the extra time I spent fixing up.

"You look beautiful." Max paused to stare some more. "Are you ready to go?"

"I'm ready, but do you think these workers will be okay without me?"

"Who, Woody G.? Absolutely. He's one guy who'll get the job done right. You don't have to look over his shoulder. By the way, we should be back by three o'clock. These guys will still be here then."

"Okay." And then we were off to our surprise

destination in Max's very high-dollar SUV. *Guess he's not after my money.* I gave myself a slap on the wrist for that thought and then let my mind unwind like a kite string on a breezy day. As I put my doubts to rest once again, my whole body began to relax. It would be a fine thing to get to know Max better. Just the two of us, discovering what made each other tick. I tried to watch him out of the corner of my eye as we rode along. He looked so different today with the sunroof open, the breeze tossing his hair. Maybe he looked happier. Hard to tell for sure.

I noticed we'd wound our way into one of the more posh areas of Houston. The homes weren't simply houses but were really well-kept mansions amid sprawling grounds. The median was lined with palm trees and pink bougainvillea. The whole neighborhood reeked of old money and privilege. *Are we eating lunch at someone else's house?*

Max pulled up in front of an enormous plantation-style home with elegant pillars. Cars lined the streets, but they mostly seemed to be concentrated around the house where we stopped. I got the sinking impression I'd been invited to a meal with his friends or relatives.

Max came around to open my door, and I eased out with a big question mark on my face. "This is an incredible house. Great location," I said like a good little Realtor. We strolled up the manicured path to the door. *Even the birds seem chirpier here. Wonder if they're on retainer.* "Now are you going to tell me what the surprise is?"

"Well, your dance card was so full, Bailey Walker, I had to seize whatever opening you had." He wiggled his eyebrows at me. "So, I brought you to my grandparents' fiftieth wedding anniversary."

Before I could protest, the double doors swung open, and I was swept into an unfamiliar world bursting with humanity, chaos, and kisses. I knew Max had a big family, but I hadn't spent much time thinking about it. Weren't his five sisters single? Who were all these people? Hordes of men, women, and children in a variety of sizes and shapes rushed up to me screaming and gushing and generally being physical and noisy. Several women asked me something, but since I couldn't make it out, I just smiled through the blare. Another wave of small fries with bobbing gold balloons and chocolate goo smeared on their faces rushed up to me. Without thinking, I raised my hands as if I'd been jumped on by a large dog.

I saw Max chuckling at me. Then he came to the rescue. "Everybody, this is Bailey." He turned back to me and took my hand. "Here's one batch of my cousins and their kids. Here's Fanny, Jane, Austen, Henry, and Edmund. Let's see, and Hart, Aileen, J.B., and John Michael. Whew."

Everybody said their hellos to me with a shout, and I waved at them all. I felt that I'd been shoved onto a stage to perform, and suddenly my skirt felt too short and my blouse too flouncey for such an affair.

"My mom came from a family of seven," Max said. "They've all had a lot of kids, so we have a bunch of cousins. Actually, I think I've lost count."

I chuckled. A weak one. I wish I could have thought of something to say. I felt like a blank page. A very crinkled blank page.

Rounds of hugs and congratulations came next. But why were they all congratulating *us*? For what? There was some sort of confusion about something. "Max," I whispered. "Why is everyone—"

"Max," one of the cousins yelled, "We're so happy for you and Bailey."

My mouth flew open, but nothing came out. Bewilderment was all I could pull out of my hat of expressions. I was sure something else would come to me eventually, but bafflement and panic were it for now.

"You see, Bailey, there's no need to hide it anymore," one of the other female cousins added. "We know your little secret with Max. He always said he would never bring a girl to one of our family get-togethers unless it was his one and only. You know, Max's bride-to-be."

Another round of hoorays rose up like a bunch of balloons. I, on the other hand, stood in stunned silence. I tried to remember how to move my mouth. My jaw remained open, and I suddenly felt as animated as a block of wood. *See, God, I knew it. This is what happens when you let people get too close. Mess.*

13

GATHERING WINDS

I wish this were a joke, but it looks too real. What kind of a date would drag an only child, who was used to a handful of people at family get-togethers to a reunion that looked like a cast of thousands on a movie set? And then add serious marital expectations to the mix! What a fandango. Unbelievable. So, what I thought would be a quiet getting-to-know-you lunch date turned out to be a trip to the circus, family-style. I rubbed my neck, but it did no good.

I shot Max an evil eye. It was the kind of penetrating look that could soften asphalt, but he wasn't paying any attention to me. He'd sunk into the quicksand of bustling kinfolk. He certainly had no look of horror or even concern over the confusion of our premarital status. In fact, he seemed to be enjoying himself immensely. But then, he's the one who'd set it up. If Max wasn't going to nip this in the bud, I'd have to correct the mix-up. "Okay," I said, trying to get the attention of the crowd. "I think I have something I need to say. We. . ."

"Of course. We are so awful to keep you to ourselves," a woman said. "Max will want you to meet his parents and then Memaw and Papaw."

The ever-stirring and chatty throng nearly carried me to what seemed to be the Grand Central Station of this hullabaloo. A mixture of aromas swirled around me of homemade pies and a zillion different perfumes. I hoped this pain behind my left eye wasn't a headache coming on. "But you don't understand. I really wanted to say—"

"Maxy!" A handsome elderly woman in green taffeta hollered to Max as she approached us. The sprightly woman with silver hair clamped her palms onto his face and planted a big kiss on his cheek. "I've missed you, Maxy. Where have you been?"

"I was at the last dinner two weeks ago." He hugged her.

"See? Too long." She waggled her head at him. "And you still owe me a game of chess."

"Anytime. I'm at your service." Max bowed low like a nobleman, making the older woman almost giggle. "Memaw. . .I want you to meet Bailey Walker."

The woman who must be Max's grandmother hugged me tightly and started to cry. She dabbed her eyes with a tissue. "Excuse me, dearie."

"I'm so sorry. Is something wrong?" I asked.

"No, my, no. These are tears of joy. I had prayed last night yet again that our Maxy would find his one and only, and God has answered my prayers." She patted me on the cheek and pulled me to her in another hug. "Bailey and Maxy. Isn't it cute? Now you go carve your initials in our big tree out back. Everybody does. It's tradition. But if our family keeps growing, I'm afraid someday we're going to kill that oak." The woman laughed with gusto."

"But Mrs. . . .I'm sorry. I don't know your last name."

The woman blew out some air and waved her hand. "No, you call me Memaw. You're family now."

"But I'm not really—"

"I know, dearie. You're not ready to raise a big family. I got panicked, too, when I was about to tie the knot. But I warmed up to the idea. Kids are such blessings. Like jewels. But I know it's a little scary seeing us all together at first. We'll grow on you. And then you'll want to have a family, too. Maxy just loves children."

Memaw was dear, but no one seemed to want to know the truth. Do all big families work that way? Talk, talk, talk, but nobody listens? I didn't know what to do, so I moved into a new phase. The Just Nodding stage. Was I angry? Yes. Was I about to make a scene? No. But a sharp-tongued woman named Bailey was about to get one Maxy Sumner off in a corner and unleash herself on him.

I accepted two more hugs from Memaw and graciously excused myself. Max must have sensed my implosion, so he took me by the elbow and steered me through the multitudes. He led me outside to a pond bordered by weeping willows. The tree's leafy tendrils floated and swayed gently in the breeze. Yes, I knew what Max was cooking. He was setting me up all right. To calm me down. To butter me up and then romance me until I couldn't resist his embrace.

I removed my arm from Max's touch. "Would you please tell me what this is all about?" I tapped my foot, but on the soft grass, it didn't have the intended challenging impact. I forced my brows together instead.

Max sat down leisurely on a tree swing beneath a massive live oak tree. He stared at me with eyes of longing. "Bailey. I honestly didn't think they'd be like bulldogs, latching onto what I'd said about my bride-to-be. I'd said it a long time ago. But that's my family. They're always looking out for each other. Supporting each other. And that's what they think they're doing. Loving me down the church aisle. They do the same thing to all my sisters since none of them have married. But I don't mind it so much, because I understand their motivation. They're family. I'm sorry if it upset you, though."

"But we're not engaged. I'm not headed down that aisle you're talking about."

"Not ever?" Max asked.

"I need lots of time to. . .examine what we have."

"Sounds kind of. . .sterile."

"But this is our first date, Max."

"I've worked side by side with you on your house for weeks now. I know you, Bailey. We have the same interests, the same faith, the same. . .attraction."

"And so you never took Priscilla to these family extravaganzas?"

"Never. None of the women I've dated. And I've dated quite a few."

"Oh, really." Well, I certainly didn't need to know that bit of trivia. I fidgeted with my ruffles, thinking they'd gotten too itchy.

"Yes. But it's been good. When you've dated a lot of women who are all wrong for you, it helps you to see the right one more clearly. Kind of like seeing one rare flower among the plain ones."

I crossed my arms and wondered if he'd hired the harpist I heard playing on the lawn. "Are you trying to charm me?"

"Is it working?" Max rose from the swing and walked toward me.

"Maybe. Although the rare-flower thing was a little over the top."

"Would it be such a horrible thing to be married to me?" Max asked.

For some reason it was hard to stay angry with Max. I knew the idea of giving him a well-deserved tongue-lashing had already slipped away. I shook my head inwardly at myself. There was no doubt. He had me in a weakened state. Was that the smell of barbeque in the breeze? *Mmm*. Now I was totally lost.

Max circled my waist with one hand while he traced my face with his finger. Just when I thought

Max was going to lean in and lay a big one on me, he released me to point out a turtle behind me. The turtle sat fat and sassy on a rock, sunning himself. Cute. But not nearly as cute as Max looked right now. I looked into his eyes and wished I could read his thoughts. Why hadn't he kissed me? Did he want me to look more eager? "Okay, you want me to say it, don't you?"

"Say what?" Max asked with what I knew dripped in pretended innocence.

"I'm supposed to ask you to kiss me. Right?"

"No. It's not necessary. But I'd like to see it in your eyes." Max grinned, but I could tell he wasn't kidding.

"I thought my eyes showed it already."

"I think you keep a lot inside, Bailey Marie," Max said.

"No one's called me Bailey Marie since Granny."

"You're changing the subject."

"I know. But I certainly wasn't hiding anything from you after I saved you last night from your fall. Remember?" I asked.

"How could I forget our first kiss? In fact, thinking about it kept me awake half the night." Max touched my hair, twirling it around his finger. "I like your hair. Auburn. It's sparkly in the light. And very soft. I like touching it."

"I was born with auburn hair, but I'm afraid the color is enhanced with what comes out of a plastic bottle in a green box. It covers my already-graying hair.

I like to keep things honest." Wonder how he'd react to them apples.

"If you're trying to scare me off, Bailey, it won't work. I don't care if you wear black orthopedic shoes and eat garlic all day."

I laughed. "Then kiss me." He'd earned it.

"And how would you like it, madam?"

My eyelashes fluttered with his request. "What? You want me to order up a kiss like a burger and fries?"

"I love your sense of humor. But, yeah, that's one way to put it."

Heat rushed to my face. Max had this way of flustering me beyond my limits. But I also didn't like shying away from his challenge. "Okay." Really, had I ever thought about this stuff before? No man had ever asked me. I guess he decided to throw me a curve, too. How did I like to be kissed? I suddenly brightened with a creative thought. I gathered my hair up. "I'd like feather-kisses right here on the back of my neck. . .for starters."

Max held my arm as he did just as I ordered, sprinkling kisses across the nape of my neck. I drifted somewhere. Not sure where. I didn't care. A tingling sensation rushed through me as he moved the kisses around to the spot right below my ear.

Max whispered, "What now?"

I suddenly felt a little audacious. "Grasp my shoulders firmly, look at me, and then kiss me until I'm breathless." I laughed at myself, because hearing those words coming out of my mouth seemed surreal.

"I wish the rest of my life were this fun," Max said as he held me firmly by my shoulders. He looked at me as if he could read my thoughts. I quickly cleaned up my mind-driftings that might be leaning toward inappropriate. Then I spotted something else in Max's eyes. Love. Not exactly what I'd asked for, but it was there in his eyes just the same. Looking at him and knowing his intentions and feelings made goose bumps spread all over me. Did he really care for me? Max leaned in and set me reeling by kissing me with the same sincere fervor he'd offered the night before. I kissed him back soundly, giving him even more distractions to keep him awake at night.

In the midst of my enchantment, I heard something offbeat. The sound of thunder growled in and out of the breeze as if the clouds had indigestion. That was normal, but something else teased the air. Between kisses I glanced toward some bushes and caught a glimpse of lemon chiffon and dainty hair ribbons. It had been the sound of a little girl giggling. . .at us! I pulled back. "Max?"

"Yes?" Max brushed my cheek with his lips as if he hadn't heard the intruder.

"I think those bushes over there have little eyes and ears."

"I know. I can hear it." Max nuzzled my neck. "I

think that's Annabel. She's always been a snoop. She got it from Aunt Dolly. Watch out for Dolly, by the way. She's our family gossip."

"But don't you mind?" I asked.

"We just get used to Dolly's inquisitiveness. It's kind of like the Spanish moss down here. You eventually just accept it as part of the tree."

"Well, what I meant is, don't you mind having kids watch us kiss?" I asked.

"Nobody has any real chunk of privacy in this family. . .especially at our big gatherings." Max released me. "But I can understand your concern if you're not used to. . .people everywhere."

"I'm not used to it at all." This time I went over and sat in the swing.

Max came behind me and pushed me until he got the swing squeaking and me laughing. "You make me feel like a kid."

"That's good. Isn't it?"

Max kept me flying until we were both aching with laughter. Max pulled me up from the swing and took my hand. "Let's walk."

It'd been a long time since I'd taken a stroll with a guy. I was used to formal dates, never just playing or wasting time with someone. The moment felt so different. So real and intimate, it made me a little uncomfortable. Formal dates could be written off so easily, but this kind of thing led to heart-sharing and closeness and commitments. I no longer had a category to file it in. Guess I might have to start a new file for Max.

"You know, I guess I've only told you a dozen times, but I think you're incredible the way you're taking that old house and making it a home."

"But you do the same thing with old houses." I said.

"Yeah. But your house was in pretty bad shape. And you weren't afraid. Coming in at night all the way from Oklahoma. You didn't know anyone. You were so courageous. Spunky like your grandmother. I admire that in you. . .as I do so many things." He brushed a strand of my hair away from my face. "You know, when you marched down the stairs that night with your hairspray can and pretended it was pepper spray, I fell in love with you right then. I can't explain it, Bailey. But I was already smitten."

I had to concentrate on his words. I'd been busy thinking about the warmth where Max was touching me on my waist. "Let me get this straight. You fell in love over that? But what if I hadn't had that little can of hairspray in my purse?"

Max laughed. "You are impossible, but adorable."

"And did you actually say the *L* word? How can you love me so easily? Love takes time. . .doesn't it? Years. My parents dated for five years before they married."

"Every couple is different, Bailey. Love comes the

way it comes. There can be no real explanations. It just happens."

"Where have I heard those words before? 'We can't create love. It happens all on its own.'" I gently moved from Max's touch. "I guess it was me who said it. . . long ago." I drew my hair behind my ears and rubbed my neck. "It's hard to imagine that coming out of my mouth."

Max took my hand again. "I don't know why I love you, Bailey. I just do." With an anxious expression, he pulled a tiny velvet box from his pocket and handed it to me. He folded his arms while he watched my reaction.

"Max, is this. . .you know. . .what I think it is?" I bit my lower lip.

"Yes."

I held the tiny box to my heart, but not without some fear. There under a weeping willow tree being whirled by the gathering winds, under a sky threatening thunderstorms, in the presence of God and angels, I held the box I knew would change the path of my life forever. If I let it. If I said yes.

I cracked open the box and saw a large diamond with a spray of smaller diamonds dancing all around the big one. The whole spectacular ring sat nestled in rich black velvet. "It's gorgeous."

Max knelt down in front of me and gathered my hands in his. "I know this may seem old-fashioned, but it's the way our family has always done it." He took a deep breath. "So here goes." He gave me an earnest look. "I love you, Bailey. I promise to cherish you always. Would you do me the honor of becoming my one and only. . .my wife?"

14

NO SWIFT ESCAPE

What you said. . .is so beautiful, Max." I looked away from all the love filling his sweet brown eyes. I hadn't felt this way in so long. I'd tried hard to forget my past. The intensity. The promise. The bright future and how it could look. And how the sting could feel when it all disappeared. "But, don't you think it's a little too soon? I'm not totally sure of the way I feel yet."

"It's probably happened more quickly for some couples and more slowly for others. I can only speak for myself," Max said smiling.

The sticky ninety-nine degrees suddenly became even more oppressive. I felt like I'd been dipped in a vat of honey and set out to gather flies. I wanted to escape from the heat and from these feelings. "But I'm not sure I can be a good homemaker. I mean, I don't even know how to thump melons."

Max rose, laughing. "I don't care. I don't need to marry a melon thumper. I need to marry the woman I love."

I turned away from him so he couldn't see my face. "But we haven't even talked about the child thing yet. Surely you don't want a passel of kids. They're so messy and loud."

"Yes, they are." Max grinned. "And I suppose *you* were always quiet and neat as a kid?"

"Yes. I *was*."

Max turned me back around to face him. "I'll bet you *were,* Miss Bailey Marie Walker."

"How do you know my middle name, anyway?"

"Your granny." Max fingered the delicate material of my blouse.

"She told you?"

"Of course. She told me a great deal about you."

I was surprised enough to frown. "And what do you think she'd say about you wanting to marry me? I mean, the contract she set up with you didn't include any of those kinds of vows."

"She would absolutely approve," Max said.

"How do you know for sure?"

"Well, I think I'd best tell you something." He stuffed his fists into his pockets like a little boy. "You see, your grandmother set up all this 'watching over you thing' just as I told you earlier. But all the time. . .she'd really hoped we'd fall in love. I warned her things don't always work out like—"

"You mean all this between us was planned? All the time when you were telling me you wanted to be my brother, you really had other designs?"

"Not exactly. *I* personally didn't think it—"

"Why didn't you just tell me the truth?" I felt my head. I surely had a big one coming on. I looked Max in the eyes. "You know, I have to tell you I'm getting a little overwhelmed here. I thought we were heading out to have a quiet getting-to-know-you-better lunch, and I find myself heading down the aisle!" I backed away from Max. "Please. Just take me home." I folded my arms, feeling deceived and a little scared. "And when we leave early, surely your relatives will know we're not engaged."

"No. They will assume we've just had a little love spat."

I handed the ring back to Max and tromped back to the house. Was all this objection on my part just a smokescreen to hide from my past and my quirky views on privacy? Or were other fears about Max raising their ugly heads again? Why did I feel so manipulated? Then I wondered if Granny had been taken in by his charms too.

"I know you love me, Bailey," Max said loudly. "You just have to admit it to yourself. In the meantime, I'll be waiting."

I grunted. Once I'd stomped up the hill, three yapping dachshunds trotted up to me. They made playful growling noises as they gnawed on my sandals and generally tried to slow me down. Why did they make me think of my three blind dates? *Bailey, you're in a vile mood, but don't get cruel.* I jiggled my feet, trying to shake off the little wiener dogs. From behind me, I could hear Max chuckling. Just as I extracted myself from the nipping, chewing dogs, a miscellaneous child wearing a suspicious color of lemon chiffon ran out from the bushes and clamped her chubby arms around my legs. She smelled like a mixture of bubblegum and wet dog.

"Aunt Bailey," the child whimpered. "Will you play ball with me? Please? Please? Please?" Her little blue eyes looked beseeching as her blond curls bounced up and down.

I didn't know what to say. But I knew I was in no mood to play any kind of game. There'd been enough games played behind my back as it was. "Well, I don't think so, hun. I'm on my way back home."

"But you just got here, Aunt Bailey." She finally let go of my legs as three more children whooshed by chasing a calico cat.

"I'm sorry." I wanted to say I didn't belong here, but I hated to see her sunny smile disappear.

"Aunt Bailey? Know what?" She smacked her gum.

Apparently the little gal wasn't deterred in the least with my refusal. "Why do you call me Aunt Bailey?"

"I heard the cousins say you were Aunt Bailey. You're the lady married to Uncle Maxy."

"No. Maxy, I mean, Max, isn't my husband. We're just friends. Sort of."

"Then why were you kissing Uncle Maxy that way? I saw you. You were real close and your mouths were touching, and I—"

"You know what, hun? Maybe when you see people kissing, it's a private thing. You—."

"My mom and dad kiss the same way, and they're married. I won't tell anybody you kissed like they do. I'm not a tattletale like Aunt Dolly. I won't tell anybody except maybe Memaw. If you get married soon, then it'll be okay. 'Cause now you'll have a baby. Do you like babies, Aunt Bailey? We have lots and lots of them around here."

I had no idea now what to say. I was back in my stunned facial phase. "Uh. Well, I guess I'd better go, sweetie."

"Know what, Aunt Bailey?"

"What?" I hope I wasn't being too sharp.

"I'll tell you a secret."

"Okay." I realized now there would be no swift escape for me. This could go on for a very long time. Did I hear thunder again? Maybe it would start pouring about now.

"I caught a garden snake in the greenhouse and put him in a jar," the girl squealed. "Do you want to see it?" Her plump fingers came together in a clap.

"No. Not right now." I tried to imagine this little girl playing with a snake in all those frothing yellow ruffles. It might actually terrify the poor snake.

"Are you 'fraid of snakes?" the girl asked.

"Only if they're poisonous. And you really have to watch out for those kind."

"I will. I promise. Would you like to name my pet?"

"No. I'll let you do it," I said.

"Then I'm going to name her Aunt Bailey 'cause she's such a nice snake and doesn't bite."

"I'm glad, sweetie. I think I need to go now. Okay? It was good to meet you."

"But you didn't really meet me. You don't know my name."

"I think you're Annabel. Right?"

"How did you know?" she asked.

"We saw you from the bushes, and Max mentioned your name."

"Oh, yeah. I was watching." She held out her hand like an adult. "I am Annabel, and it is so very good to meet you."

I shook her small, warm hand. Then Annabel wiggled and spun around, letting her ruffled undergarments show. I wasn't sure what her little dance was for, but it made her laugh. Maybe kids did it to discharge surplus energy.

"When will you come back? I want you to come back." Annabel chattered as she picked her nose.

"I don't know." I guess her mother hadn't been 100 percent successful in coaching her in the rules of etiquette.

"We're going to have another party in two weeks. It's Papaw's birthday," Annabel said. "You can't miss it, 'cause we're going to have a magic man come and somebody who makes funny balloon animals. I could have him make a snake. A balloon snake would be easy to make, wouldn't it, Aunt Bailey?" The girl shook all over with giggles.

"Yes, you're right. But, no, I don't think I'll be here for the party. I'm sorry." I hadn't talked to children in so long, I'd forgotten how exhausting it could be. I felt as if someone had beaten me with a mallet.

"Too bad you're not coming to the party. 'Cause I like you, Aunt Bailey." Then the little gal in the lemon chiffon hugged my legs again. My eyes filled with mist, but I blinked hard enough to stop the flow. This was no time to go all mushy.

I glanced back down the path. Max sat on the grass watching the whole thing as if it were a stage play. He'd apparently heard and seen it all. I hugged the girl and said my good-byes. As I walked away, she said, "I know you'll come back."

"How do you know?" I asked.

"'Cause you are Uncle Maxy's one and only," Annabel said.

What a heart tug. But could Max have paid her to say all this? I waved good-bye to Annabel and then headed toward the house with a purposeful stride. As I passed the plucking harpist playing some sentimental tune, the lawn seemed to come alive with children of every age. I wondered if the air or water was teeming with something. I found myself holding my breath.

Everything all around looked so lush and verdant. The flowers burst with ripe color, the abundant trees seemed, well, abundant. What a fertile house.

A headache had arrived. Full force. *Oh, dear God, how could You have ever led me here? Maybe I got my wires crossed and didn't hear You right. Maybe I should have sold Granny's house and stayed in Oklahoma. Show me the way, God, because I think I took a wrong turn somewhere.*

Just then Max came up behind me and touched my back. He once again steered me through the crowds with all the right words. Two people did make a comment about a love spat, but Max just laughed them off. I had long since given up on correcting them, so I just let him do the leading as I did the following.

I realized once we were in the car that he hadn't introduced me to his parents or grandfather. I guess I'd made it clear it didn't matter. But still, I wondered what they were like. If Max looked like his mom or his dad. Would they have liked me? *What am I thinking?* I have just what I'd asked for—a drive back to the house.

Home, even my old house, would feel good. So quiet and peaceful after such a fiasco. But silence came early, because it ruled while I rode home in Max's SUV. When he dropped me off, I saw discontent in his eyes, and it made me grieve to think I'd been the one to put it there. He made no effort to kiss me and no effort to continue to convince me to marry him.

"I'll see you later," Max finally said.

I stayed on the porch and watched him go. The moment had a forlorn and final feel to it as he walked away. A feel I didn't like one bit. The hurt had already started.

Woody G. and the crew waved down at me. The house was really shaping up and starting to look like home, at least on the outside. So I faked a smile and fumbled inside to the seclusion I apparently craved above all else. I sat in my kitchen on one of my hard metal chairs and wanted to cry but didn't. The hush of the house sounded like a tomb, not my peaceful oasis. Now the gift of being alone felt more like a prison term than privacy. Max had ruined me. I'd never enjoy my sweet solitude again.

What am I doing? Really? Do I care about this man who stormed into my corner of the world because of Granny? Am I chucking one of the most important things in my life just because I can't cope with giving myself away? Trusting again? Or perhaps I still hadn't let go of something else—something more disturbing. But I no longer wanted my mind to play in that park of sinister ideas concerning Max. A churchgoing man who had such a sweet Memaw could not have a criminal mind.

But what about his whole family, which was the size of a nomadic tribe? There'd be fertility demands. What if I were sterile? Couldn't produce offspring? *Barren* has got to be an obscene word in his family. I would be an utter outcast. Would it then force Max to look elsewhere? It seemed like a reasonable question.

Or what if I were ultrafertile and just didn't know it yet—a mother-in-waiting with an incubator capable of a whole litter of snotty-nosed infants? Did I want a pack of kids spreading germs, noise, and bodily fluids all over *my* house? But it would cease to be *my* house. It would be *our* house. What a foreign concept. But I had always known there was the chance of marriage. I just hadn't expected to wed a small country and produce one as well.

And what about the living arrangements? Whose house would we live in? Would I have to give up my home after all this work? I remember Max mentioning a female family gossip named Dolly. Would she run our lives? Would our house be the new Grand Central? And what about all the nosiness from the sisters and other family members? Everyone would know my business. My thoughts. My inner life. My outer life. My comings and goings. It would send me to distraction. *Maybe I should say good-bye now.* End it before the real pain begins. But how do you say good-bye to a guy who lives only yards from your front door?

I slapped my forehead in utter frustration. And I hadn't even pondered the concept of manipulation. Is that what Granny and Max were up to? Or was it all much more innocent. A genuine concern for me?

Yet again, too many questions. Never enough

answers. The story of my life. I rubbed my neck and felt like doing something crazy. Like eating an entire carton of Muddy Fudge ice cream. Or buying some outrageously gaudy costume jewelry. Or watching movies until I got serious eyestrain. Except I no longer owned a TV or DVD player, since I sold off my belongings before coming to Houston. Or maybe I could put a FOR SALE sign in the front yard. It would solve a lot of my problems. But I hated just to run away. I'd always think of myself as a coward.

I glanced at my watch. Oh no. Guess those reflections would have to be placed on hold. Apparently, according to the time, I soon had a blind date with a guy named Rupert. Why had I said yes? Why was Dedra so anxious for me to date? Did I look desperate? And if Rupert was so wealthy and wonderful, why wasn't he already married by now? Something smelled like rotten mackerel.

Or maybe Rupert was simply a guy who never found his one and only. Did Max really call me that? My heart warmed, and I felt I was betraying him by continuing to go on these blind dates. But I'd made a promise, so I wasn't going to cancel. Oh well, they'd be over soon.

After a speedy shower, I slid on a plain tan skirt and a white knit top. The doorbell sounded. *Please, God, let this go well. Or at least let us not be miserable.* The latter prayer seemed more realistic.

I opened the door to Blind Date Number Two. "Hi.

You must be Rupert." He stood before me without the slightest Greek angle but instead had more the rounded look of a face that had been thrown into a rock tumbler. Tufts of black hair jutted up on his head as if he were receiving UFO signals. Guess the wind was picking up outside. Other than those imperfections, Rupert had adorable dimples when he smiled, making him endearing and cute. Maybe I could put him on a leash. *Bailey, stop trying to sabotage this date before it begins. I think I'm forming a pattern here, and all the lines lead to Max. I can see the way more clearly every day and with every date. Max, I miss you.*

"Yes. I'm Rupert Rutledge. And I presume you are Bailey Walker, whom I've heard so much about."

15

DISSECTING AIR

In the end, I was grateful Rupert didn't ask me out again. Maybe we both sensed we would be better off just living our lives apart—far apart preferably. All in all, though, Dedra had been right. He was a good Christian man. He just wasn't the good Christian man meant for me. Funny how one can mix in all the right ingredients and still not make an edible cake. *Goodbye, Rupert. I wish you well. And I thank you. Knowing you has helped me to see a few things more clearly.*

The next morning my alarm went off, and I think I made a snorting sound as I woke up. Hard to tell. I gave the noisy machine a slam-dunk into the trash basket. I knew I'd have to dig the silly thing out later, but it was gratifying to give it the old slap and toss. I turned my mental motor off again and coasted back down the hill to nocturnal bliss.

When the sun became too bright to ignore, I threw back my covers in an act of resignation and jammed my tootsies into my powder blue scuffies. I wiggled my toes in the softness. Shoes like clouds. I'd be all right now, especially since the two-way radio on my bed table had never made another sound. There'd been no more break-ins or scary incidents. No more hazy figures running across my lawn. No more analyzing bits of vague suspicions like I was dissecting air. Except for missing Max, life was good again.

I stretch. I yawned. I breathed in the stale air. And then I remembered. Another blind date. Oh, well, at least the torture would be over soon. Who was the guy? Oh yeah. Lee somebody. Another friend of Dedra's from church.

Church! Oh, no. I looked at my watch on the table. The last service had already started. I sighed. *God, forgive me. Next Sunday I'll be back in sync.*

I slipped on my chenille robe and stared out the window, relieved there were no workmen hammering on my house on Sunday.

I surveyed the neighborhood, noticing the curious combo of trees. Would I ever get used to seeing pines, oaks, and palm trees together? Somewhere a mourning dove cooed. I loved that sound. Melancholy but soothing.

And then I saw the same elderly couple I'd seen before—my other next-door neighbors. The woman actually wore a headscarf in this heat! She appeared to be arguing with her husband. They looked none too happy with life or each other. Suddenly, they pointed toward my house. For some reason, I stepped away out of their sight. Not sure why I would do that. Gut reaction. What were their names again? Oh, yeah. Boris and Eva Lukin. Max had called them cantankerous. *I wonder what their story is. Should I run down to meet them?* They looked too angry for a neighborly chitchat. The couple lumbered off and disappeared behind a row of oleanders. Were they hiding again? Who knew?

I headed to the bathroom, thinking of my next, and final, blind date. A lunch date with a man named Lee Yorker. Dedra said he was a nice Christian guy who loved eating out in many of Houston's finest restaurants. *Hmm. Yorker rhymes with Porker. Hope that isn't some kind of sign.*

So with a leisurely tempo, I showered and slapped on what I've dubbed my "number two painted face." Applying makeup is mostly a waste of valuable time, but I discovered in today's society it's a necessary evil. So I've conformed. And over the years, for speed and convenience, I'd developed three faces for going out. A number one face is my makeup job for everyday routines like going to the grocery store, clothes shopping, or running out for a quick bite of lunch. My number two face is the next level up, used for generic dates, church functions, and business dealings.

My number three face. . .well, it rises to the maximum primping level and is only brought out for very special occasions. I had to think about it. Didn't do many of those number threes. It took extra time, such as eyebrow plucking, dramatic and dimensional eye shadow application, and sparkling bronze powder on all exposed upper body parts. This dusting procedure sets my face like a Mardi Gras mask, but hopefully not including the nightmarish expression.

I guess since I'd been in Houston, the only date that merited my number three face was. . .Max. Once again, my mind drifted over to his house, but after a moment of lingering there, I tucked my dreams away. . .for now.

Even if I chose never to marry, I knew God could show me ways to fill my home with love and ways to share that joy with others. I wasn't there yet, but somehow God saw potential in me like a precious stone stuck in the dirt. I felt a prayer coming on. *Oh God, whatever it takes, I really need You to show me the way.* Could Max possibly be my one and only? Knowing God has a sense of humor and remembering how He'd put me on quite an eye-popping roller-coaster ride recently, I wondered what my prayer might unleash.

After completing my number two face, I headed down to the row of hard chairs in my living room. I flipped through a magazine. It was like living in a doctor's office.

Then suddenly the wet chamois of reality slapped me across the face. The doorbell had rung, which meant Lee Yorker was now waiting for me on the other side of that door. He'd come early. I raised an eyebrow. Anxious, I guess.

I made my peek, flipped the deadbolt, and opened up to the world of my third blind date. Mr. Lee Yorker anointed me with his dashing good looks and killer smile. *Dresses well. Doesn't have a goofy grin. Major points for that one. Okay. What's wrong? There has to be something wrong with this guy. Probably the only thing wrong is. . .he isn't Max.* I offered my hand to him. "Hi. I'm Bailey. It's nice to meet you."

Lee smoothed his blond hair back, looked at me, and then took my hand. He brought my fingers up to his mouth and kissed them with warm lips. The gesture was so immediately intimate, I shivered with concern. Was he from another culture where this was acceptable? Was he being theatrical for fun? But why? What was the matter with this guy?

Then another tremor of a different kind coursed through me. Was there such a thing as déjà vu with touch? If so, this was it. Amazingly, the contact with Lee felt familiar somehow. The way he kissed my hand. And those eyes—I somehow knew that startling color of ocean blue. Who was this stranger? I had the feeling it was not Lee Yorker. My hand shriveled away from his grasp. "Who are you. . .really?"

"I'm sorry," the stranger said. "I didn't mean to scare you. I've come so far—"

"You must not be Lee. Who are you?" My eyes narrowed.

"Who's Lee?" The stranger sounded offended.

"I'd say under the circumstances, it's none of your business. Please tell me who you are. Do I know you?"

"Bailey. Don't you recognize me? Your old fiancé?

I know it's been a long time, and well, my hair's lighter now, but I haven't changed that much. Have I?"

My hand flew to my forehead. I gasped. "Sam. Is it you?" I felt lightheaded.

16

Loose-Tongued Lily

I t's me." Sam tried to pull me into a lover's embrace.
"No," I said. "Please." *What a nightmare. I only
wish I could wake up from it.*

Sam pulled back. "Aren't you glad to see me?" He
appeared stunned at my reaction.

I winced and shook my head, not for any dramatic
effect, but from his audacious behavior. The moment
was like a hard fall—sharp pain mixed with shock. "To
be honest, the last time I saw you. . .it was a bit strange.
I was watching from a parked car as you escorted your
new bride to your limo."

"You were actually watching us?" Sam chuckled.

"Pathetic, isn't it. . .what love does?"

Sam lowered his head. "It must have been rough
on you."

I stared at this male figure who'd once been a big part
of my life—the man who'd wrapped his heart around
mine, promised to marry me—only to break that same
heart when he ran away with my best friend, Annie.

Sam Hunter had changed some. He'd grown older,
but he was still striking. Tall and tanned and always
flashing those baby blues of his around like he ruled
the world.

"I've missed you, babe." Sam gave me a glance up and down. "And look at you. You haven't changed a bit. Maybe a little crow's-feet, but you're still looking trim and pretty." He snapped his fingers as he hit his fist into his palm.

I remember Sam used to make that gesture when he felt as if he'd won at something. "This conversation is not only insulting, it's inappropriate. You're married to Annie. Your choice has been made."

"No. It's been over for a while now. Actually, I think it was over the day we married." Sam frowned as he stared at me. "Annie and I have been divorced for six months now." He shuffled his feet. "She left me for another guy. Somebody with a political future. I think she fancies herself becoming a senator's wife someday. She always liked the limelight. Remember? Always up on stage wanting all the attention. I should have seen it coming." He let out a chuckle, but it faded into a choking sound.

"I'm sorry. I know how that can hurt." I wasn't going to lower myself by mentioning how he'd sledge-hammered my heart to bits. Although every pore of my body wanted to.

"Yes. I guess you *would* know," Sam said.

"I thought I'd heard you were out in California. Did you move to Houston?" I certainly hoped that wasn't the case.

"No. I came here just to see you. One of those

Realtors where you used to work in Oklahoma City told me you were moving to Houston."

"Oh." *Probably Loose-Tongued Lily.*

"Listen. Do you mind if we take this little reunion inside? It's kind of steamy out here. By the way, how can you stand this humidity? And what are you doing in this ugly old house? This is *so* not you."

I straightened my shoulders. "Sam, I don't think coming in would be wise. . .under the circumstances."

"Why not? I'm not married."

Sam tilted his head and raised one side of his lip. An expression I used to think was endearing. "I moved on, Sam. I had to find a way to make a life for myself. One that didn't include you. But I suppose I should thank you, because when I ran away from the pain, I ran toward God."

"Come on, now. I was never big on all the redemption stuff. Whenever I've been delivered from anything, it was by using my own wit. I just sort of went along with you back then, but I've determined over the years it's a waste of time. There're so many more important things to do."

"Like what?"

Sam leaned in on the door frame, trying to look amorous, but appeared sleazy instead. "Well, now that you bring it up."

I got a whiff of his cologne. Musky, but overpowering enough to make my nostrils burn. I coughed. Not the reaction he'd hoped for, I'm sure.

"And as I recall," Sam said as he leered at me, "you always had other qualities that took up my time. That never changes, babe."

No more! I will not get sucked into this guilt trip. The intimacies I'd shared with Sam were long since forgiven. Transgressions tossed away as far as east was from west. It was His promise, and so if God Almighty wasn't going to make me wallow in the muck, then neither was Sam. Now, I just pitied him. Sam seemed lost in so many ways. I wondered when his cheerful confidence had turned to such cocky behavior. Had Annie done this to Sam, or had he always been arrogant and I just couldn't see it? But I saw him clearly now as he destroyed all illusions I'd ever had of seeing him as my champion. I said a quick prayer for courage. "I want you to leave. Please."

"Come on now. I don't have time for these games," Sam said with an edge to his voice.

I decided not to respond to his bullying and simply raised my chin.

Sam raised his chin higher than mine. "I'm not leaving."

"It would be a shame to call the police, especially since you're an officer yourself."

Sam shook his head. "I left the department. I'm a private detective now."

I softened my frown. "Sam. This isn't going to

work between us. Surely you can see it."

"Please." Sam reached out to stroke my arm.

I pulled away, hoping he'd finally get the message.

Then Sam slipped past me into the entryway. "Just let me have a peek inside."

"Sam. No." I stayed in the doorway, waiting for him to come back.

He circled the front rooms, mumbled something derogatory, and then strolled back to the front door. "There. That wasn't so bad. I just wanted to see how you were living. To be honest, I've seen you with better accommodations."

"Well, this house certainly looks better than my apartment after it was trashed." I wasn't going to get pulled into the past, and yet it bubbled up in spite of my resolve.

"Oww. Bailey, sweetheart. You do still care for me, or you wouldn't get riled up so easily."

"You're taking it the wrong way. I wish I hadn't brought it up. I don't want to argue with you. Or even to discuss the past."

"I'm disappointed in you. I thought you'd at least invite me in for some coffee. You've lost all your warmth and kindness."

"I'm sorry I let you down." I tried to keep the sarcasm out of my voice.

"Won't you ever forgive me?" Sam said with fake sweetness.

"I don't think that's why you're here. To ask me for forgiveness."

Sam let a slow grin spread across his face. "You still know my ways. *You're* what I really need. In fact, babe, it's difficult being so close to you like this and—"

"Please stop." I remembered just after Sam and Annie became engaged, I'd still believed Sam would come to his senses. I'd waited for a moment just like this one. But now we were truly worlds apart. *Oh Lord, forgive me for making such a foolish choice back then, and thank You for Your hedge of protection.* I wanted Sam to be very clear about my intentions. "I'm sorry you've come so far, and I'm truly sorry about Annie, but what I felt for you years ago. . .is gone. So I'm asking you one more time to please go. Now." Did he notice the little shake in my voice? Was someone coming up the walk?

Sam suddenly looked around and frowned.

The man, who must certainly be Lee, moved in cautiously. "Hi. I'm Lee Yorker. I hope I'm not inter-rupting something here."

Sam narrowed his eyes. "Well, as a matter of fact—"

"Actually, Sam had stopped by. But I think we've covered everything we needed to cover," I said in a businesslike tone. I turned back to Sam. "I wish. . .no, I *pray* the very best for you." I stuck out my hand to Sam, but this time he backed away. I saw genuine sadness in his eyes. And something else. A somewhat restrained but palpable look of vengeance.

17

THE GRISLY SPECTACLE

O kay. I'll go," Sam said as he brushed by Lee and
off the porch. "But I will be back. . .Bailey. Do
you hear me?" He shot me another loaded look and
strode to his car in silence.

I let out the breath I'd been holding. I wanted to
end the farce and tell him once again the relationship
was over, but I figured hollering that kind of soap-
opera language to Sam might not be the best way to
start my date with Lee.

"I'm sorry I broke up your conversation," Lee said.

"I do apologize." I looked at Lee. He appeared kind,
his green eyes warm and merry. *And what was the word?
Guileless.* Yes, I was in need right now of some guilelessness.
He smelled clean and fragrant like a grove of pine trees.
Not bad. His only flaw was his hair, which was gelled
within an inch of its life. It reminded me of the molded
plastic hair on the dolls I played with as a girl—the kind
of mane that was never meant to be disturbed. Ever. Sort
of hair with rigor mortis. But Lee seemed like a saint
compared to Sam, so I filed my critical nature away and
pulled something out of the Bailey-needs-to-lighten-up
drawer. "This was totally unexpected," I said. "Sam just

showed up. I'm so sorry."

"Old flame?" Lee asked.

"Yes. I'm afraid so. *Very* old. And the flame is out."
How odd to share such personal data with a stranger.

I smiled at Lee as we trotted down the sidewalk to his
blue sedan. Just as he pulled out, I saw a huge black bird
on the street hopping around and picking at something.
The bird shot a piercing glance my way and then went
back to his meal. The vulture, a rather prehistoric looking
creature, tore at the flesh of a dead squirrel. His head
appeared bald but radiated the same color as the intestines
he was eating. I thought a dry heave might be in order but
decided to look away and cringe instead.

Lee seemed oblivious to the grisly spectacle, so I
didn't bother pointing it out. If you could bottle this
feeling, it would do well on the market as an appetite
suppressant. I tried to dismiss the scene, which, oddly
enough, felt a lot like my episode with Sam.

Later that afternoon, I arrived home in one piece
physically but not emotionally. No matter how determined I was not to think about Sam, the incident still left
an unsettled place in my spirit.

Lee had been great and indeed guileless. As fine a
man as Dedra had promised. But even if I'd agreed to
have another date with him, we both knew our time
together hadn't truly clicked. Lee was handsome and
witty and sane. That last one was always a real plus. But
there'd been no enchantment. No parallel passions. No

sense of eagerness and wonder. I knew he felt the same. People can just sense these things.

My excursion into the dating scene had once again felt like being on a merry-go-round. When I was a kid I wanted to throw up after going too many rounds, but now I didn't feel nauseated, just weary. Interesting about dates. Witty things can be said, scrumptious food can be shared, fun can be had, and the entire experience can even appear textbook perfect. . .but still not satisfy. Not like Max. I hated to compare, but it was impossible not to. Even good men didn't hold up well when put side by side with Max.

I puttered around the kitchen for a while, putting on a pot of coffee. As the water began to drip through the grounds, my musings filtered back to Sam. So much time had passed. So much pain and betrayal. Why would he think he could start back up with me as if nothing had transpired? Was it a macho thing or just a human thing? I simply wanted Sam to leave. Leave Houston and go back to California where he could live out his sad, sorry life, making someone else's life miserable. *Oh God, make my thoughts pleasing, because I'm certainly not feeling very compassionate right now.*

But I couldn't help wondering why I'd been so enamored with Sam. So utterly captivated, I was no more than an android waiting for instructions from the mother ship. I'd been blind, and my loss of discernment troubled me.

Could I somehow be blinded again? Could Max be another Sam, only I wouldn't realize it until it was too late? These were the complex truths rising to the surface of this scum-covered day. Sam certainly didn't make me want to run into his arms. And now that I thought more about it, Sam didn't make me want to run into Max's arms either. The whole episode just made me want to run.

Oh God, how can bringing Sam to Houston be a part of Your plan to show me the way? I know You've taken care of my house, my finances, and my friends, so I should be trusting You. . .but Sam is just muddying the water and messing with my head. I guess the Bible speaks truth when it reads, "His ways are not my ways."

After pouring myself a large mug of French roast, I loaded down my brew with heaping tablespoonfuls of sugar and whipped cream. I needed the extra reinforcement. The mixture must have awakened a sixth sense, because I suddenly made a connection I hadn't thought of before. Sam said he'd left the department to become a private detective, but had he really been dismissed from the force? And would all the sudden rejections in his life make him eager for revenge? On anyone?

As I turned toward the back door, an image caught my attention. There on my largest kitchen window was a shimmery *w* drawn on the pane of glass. As fast as a bullet from a rifle, I thought, "I've seen this image before." A lowercase *w*, reminding me of the top of a pitchfork. The icon on the window glared back at me as if issuing a challenge. But then maybe Woody G.'s crew had to scribble the *w* on the window as some kind of instruction to the crew. Or was the perpetrator of this gibberish the same person who destroyed the cat, impaled the butterfly, and left the two-way radio in my backyard?

I ran my hand over the glass and was relieved to find that the drawing had been made from the outside. No one could get in now. I had accomplished my goal with my tight security. But still someone out there lingered, wanting to tell me something. Wanting to tease me, or scare me, or worse.

I leaned in more closely to the design and noticed it didn't really look drawn on, but actually etched into the surface. So, I wouldn't be able to just wash it off. I'd actually have to replace the pane of glass. I knew now Woody G.'s men wouldn't have deliberately damaged the window. Max had recommended them highly, and they'd already done a great job.

Then I remembered the heated look in Sam's eyes as he walked away. The tiniest trembling started at the back of my neck and ran down my spine. The heebie-jeebies made me shiver all over just like when I was little, but I wasn't a child anymore, and this didn't really seem like playground antics. I rubbed my arms. But why would Sam choose a message that was so cryptic? Wouldn't he want to witness my reaction? Or was he watching me now, and I just didn't know it?

I pressed in on my temples to release the pounding in my head. If Sam were indeed behind all the trouble, I could ignore him. I wouldn't open the door to him again, and if Sam chose not to leave the front porch, I could call the police. He'd always had a temper, and he certainly had no problem with breaking and entering or vandalism when it came to my apartment, but would he be capable of crimes more evil in nature? Capable of. . .murder?

I heard a scratching on the window and jerked backward. Oh. Only a branch tapping against the glass. *Getting kind of jumpy, aren't you, Bailey?* I decided to mention the damaged window to Woody G. so he could replace it right away. Trying to relax, I took a deep swig of my coffee and then licked off my whipped cream mustache. Maybe I'd read for a while.

Later that evening, my head still pounded, so I took an aspirin and dropped into bed. I waited for the house to start its usual symphony of pops and creaks. I wondered if I'd stay in the house until I was so old that my moaning joints would be louder than the house's. What a thought.

I looked over at Liberty, my faithful beta fish. He gawked at me from his watery world with a bloated expression. I did the unforgivable and tapped on the glass. Was he dead? *Wishful thinking?* No. I loved beta. Sort of. As much as you can love an aquatic being who's not very responsive or snuggly. I looked again. No, Liberty was fine. He was just being a beta.

I fluffed my feather pillow and sank down into its downy delight. Moments later, I felt the night fairies tickling me with their wings. I got really sleepy in spite of all my swirling thoughts and worries.

I woke up with a start as if my heart were taking off on a launching pad. Did I hear the doorbell? The radiance of the daylight had drenched every crevice of the room. What happened? Did I forget to set the alarm? Was Woody G. at the door with more questions about the repairs and painting? I pulled the covers back and jumped into action. I gathered my hair up with a large clip, threw on jeans and a T-shirt, and ran downstairs.

Because of the incident with Sam the previous day, I took a good look through the peephole. Dedra leaned in so close to the eyehole, she resembled an ogress.

"I know you're in there, you rascal," Dedra hollered.

Yeah. I knew what she wanted—a play-by-play of the blind dates. I opened the door. "Hi, there." I said noncommittally.

Dedra stood before me as if she were headed to Woodstock. All she needed was a wreath of baby's breath on top of her braided hair and a guitar over her shoulder. She put her hands on her hips. "Okay. I need blind date facts and some French roast. Pleeease. By the way, I missed you at church yesterday."

"Yes, I'm very sorry about that." I squinted in the

light. "Do you realize what time it is?"

"Yeah. Eight-thirty and time to get up." Dedra tapped her watch and grinned.

She was right. "I'm getting so lazy. What is the matter with me?"

"It's called, 'you had such a great time, you just needed a little extra rest.' Let's go, Baileyo. Cough up the details." She smiled.

"Forgive me, but I ran out of coffee, and the news isn't promising." I placed an affable grin on the top of my pile of negatives to soften the blow. "But please come in." I decided not to tell her about the most recent incidents, such as the damaged window.

Suddenly, a teenager ambled up the walk with a bouquet of yellow roses. I'd wondered why there was a florist's van parked in front of my house.

"Happy anniversary," the young man said with gusto, making his cowlick wobble.

"Hi. I think you must have the wrong house. I'm not even married."

The young stranger had a big question mark on his face. "You're Bailey Walker? Right?"

"That's me."

"Well, these are for you then. Oh. The customer requested that I read the card to you." He pulled off the note attached to the bouquet. "It says, 'Happy anniversary. It's your first month in your new house. May your home always be filled with friendship, love, and laughter.'"

"Did the card say who sent them?" I prayed the flowers weren't from Sam.

"No name on the card," the teen said. "But it does say, 'From Your One and Only.'"

Dedra eyed me. "Oh, so there's juice you're not letting me sip."

I shot her a friendly smirk and then handed the kid a tip.

"Thanks for the twenty." He winked at me. "I've got four more of these bouquets in the van. . .for you. It's a good day, right?"

"Right." I got wide-eyed like a small child at Christmas. I waved my hands like an idiot. *Good grief, woman. You're acting like you've never received flowers in your life.* Actually, I couldn't even remember the last time a man had sent me flowers. And certainly never so extravagantly.

Dedra shook her head. "Yeah. You've been holding out on me, big time. So, who is this guy? I mean, he nearly cleaned out a florist shop for you."

I paused, but I knew Dedra wouldn't stand for any more hesitation. "Okay. It's Max." It sounded good coming out of my mouth.

"Oh my. I guess that would be true. I've seen the way you two look at each other." Dedra hugged me, but a bit of the spark had left her smile.

"I haven't said yes."

"You mean he asked you. . .to marry him?" Dedra said. "Really?"

"Yes." I bit down on my lip. I could hardly believe it. "He did ask me." I suddenly remembered Dedra had once dated Max, but their relationship hadn't worked out. Did she still care for him? Is that why she tried so hard to set me up with other people? I prayed the news wouldn't cause her to spiral down into a depression. I knew so little about bipolar disorder, I wasn't sure what to say.

"Is everything okay?" I asked with concern. "You seem a little—"

"I'm fine. Really. I just have a little indigestion from a strange combination of foods I just ate. You know prunes and whipped cream and chili don't mix."

I shuddered, making Dedra laugh. After a few minutes, she perked back up as we situated the bouquets of flowers around the room. The sight looked like either a wedding or a wake. I chuckled to myself as I touched the silky petals. What a heady aroma. I'd forgotten how good roses could make me feel. *Oh, Max. How did you know yellow roses were my favorite?* I didn't even know they were my favorite.

"Did you read all the cards?" Dedra asked.

"No. I guess I thought there was just the one." I noticed another card sticking up out of the profusion of yellow and green. "It says, 'I would be honored if you would allow me to pick you up at ten o'clock today for an outing I've planned for us. No crowds. No relatives. Formal attire suggested. Max.'"

Dedra whistled. "Now is that romantic, or what?"

I waggled my head in agreement. I guess that meant I was going on another date with Max. My goodness. Sucked in by yellow roses and sweet nothings. I couldn't seem to help myself.

"Bailey?" Dedra touched my shoulder.

"Yeah?" I wasn't sure how long my thoughts had been ruminating on Max.

"Don't you think you should start getting ready?" she asked. "Like right now?"

"Yes. I suppose I should. Especially since it's formal. Guess I'll wear my black dress. It's the only formal one I have. Except for a flowery turquoise gown from a wedding. . .about ten years ago. . .which makes me look like a floral sofa."

"I'd go with the black dress," Dedra said without hesitation.

I nodded.

"I think I'll go now." Dedra raised her eyebrows as she walked to the door. "I want a full accounting. Okay?"

"All right." I tilted my head at her. "Thanks. For being my friend." *Did those words actually come out of my mouth? Incredible.*

"You're welcome."

Sadness still seemed to linger in Dedra's eyes. If she did still care for him, I felt badly to say the least. Would I have gone out with Max had I known the depth of her feelings? Was it one more reason for me to say good-bye to him? I certainly understood her heartache, since my best friend had married the man I'd loved. Of course, the circumstances were different with Max and Dedra since years had passed, but it might not feel much differently in her heart. After I hugged her good-bye, I prayed for Dedra again, asking God to give her strength and joy as well as a peace and soundness in her mind. I also asked God to help Dedra find her one and only.

Later I pounded my way upstairs, wondering if Dedra's ailment really had been indigestion—wondering if I had once again chosen to see things that weren't there.

I shook my head at my own ineptness at being a human being and then turned my attention to making myself as elegant as a thirty-year-old woman could be. I carefully placed my number three face into position and swirled my hair up with tiny silver clasps. I slipped into my little black dress with the thin shoulder straps. And I added some dangly diamond earrings, which looked good with Granny's necklace.

I wondered if people could wear such formal attire before six o'clock. I'm sure some etiquette guru had cooked up a rule on it somewhere. But Max had said formal dress. And besides, I was in a diamonds-on-black kind of mood.

I sat reading the end of my mystery novel, *Where There's Smoke*, as I waited for Max. Were my hands perspiring? Maybe I needed to lower the thermostat on my air units. I waved my hands, trying to dry them. Funny how I had never had to fan my hands before the other dates.

A Fading Dream

The bell chimed exactly at ten, and this time I looked forward to opening the door.

"Hi, there," Max said. He stood before me in a black tux and a grin that set my heart into a schoolgirl flutter.

I took in a short breath of air and noticed a white stretch limo waiting for us by the curb. I carefully secured the house and turned back to Max.

He took in his own quick breath. "You look. . . gorgeous."

"Thank you. You do, too."

Max laughed. What a wonderful sound. I circled my arm through his as we headed down the walkway. Once again, I decided to set my smorgasbord of worries aside. "Do you mind if I ask what the special occasion is? I thought Priscilla said you weren't the tux type."

Max's eyes filled with tenderness. And maybe a touch of wonder, too. "Well, I guess she just didn't inspire me."

What a great line. If it'd come from anyone else, I would have thought it too smooth. But not Max. Everything about him appeared earnest. It was hard to do anything but enjoy his company and taste paradise. And his cologne wasn't bad either. Woodsy and light. "I'm also curious about something else."

"Yes?"

"Why are we going out so early?"

"Because I couldn't wait another hour to see you." Max kissed my hand.

I raised an eyebrow. *That answer gets an A+.*

An older man sporting an official-looking hat opened one of the limo doors for us.

"Thanks, Jarrett. Hey, I want you to meet someone very special." Max made the introductions. "By the way, I like your jacket. It's new, isn't it?" he asked Jarrett.

"Yes." Jarrett winked. "It's Italian."

"I can tell. Well, you can afford it," Max said.

Jarrett's face broke into an agreeable grin, which, I noted, seemed to radiate not only pleasantness but also a gentle strength. His skin, the color of rich mahogany, glowed youthfully in spite of the deep wrinkles. I became curious as to the relationship between the two men. They appeared to have a close friendship.

Jarrett shut our door, closing us into a lavish cocoon. I scooted farther into the cushy belly of the vehicle. The leather looked like softened butter, and there appeared to be enough legroom for a pair of pampered camels.

After giving instructions to Jarrett, Max pressed his hand over mine.

The weather had been hot, but somehow the temperature suddenly rose another ten degrees. I hoped I wasn't already perspiring in my dress. "So, where are we headed?" I asked.

"Certainly not a family party. Just you and me, kid."

"Okay." I relaxed my shoulders and caught myself squeezing his hand back. I let the posh surroundings enfold me. "By the way, thanks for the roses. They're so many and so lovely. What made you pick yellow?"

"It just seemed like the right color."

"They were the perfect color." Perfect because Max had bought them and sent them.

"So, I guess you've forgiven me for turning my relatives loose on you?"

I nodded and then reached up to touch his cheek, fascinated at how I'd surrendered my doubts so easily. He turned my hand over and kissed my palm. That simple gesture felt soothing and stirring all at the same time. I knew we were seconds away from a kiss, and the anticipation was almost as exciting as I knew the actual contact would be.

Max simply kissed me on the forehead but continued to hold my hand. "I think we'd better not get started too early." His warm breath ruffled the tendrils of hair around my face. "I'm having a difficult time as it is just being so close to you, babe."

Did I hear him right? Those were almost the exact

same words Sam had just said to me. And "babe"? Max never used that word.

"Is something wrong?" he asked. "You look ill."

I shook my head and leaned against him, not wanting to say anymore.

Max pulled me close, but all my nagging fears rose up again, threatening to tear me away from him. *What am I to do?* Then two questions came to me clearly— how long would I punish myself by sacrificing love for fears that were unfounded, and how long would I continue to rebuke Max for the sins of another man? Is that what I'd been indulging in?

Outside the window, the world and all its activities seemed to whirl by us in time-lapse photography. I eased away from Max a little, feeling a surprising need to talk—to tell him more about my past. "I want to tell you something."

"What is it?"

I fingered Granny's necklace. "As you already know, I've been a private sort of person for a long time." As Max held my hand, I told him the story of Sam and Annie. And then I shared about my dear family and their home-going to heaven.

Max shook his head with such a sad expression. "It must be hard for you to have any confidence in me," he said. "You must assume I'm either going to die right away or leave you."

"Well, my life hasn't been a tea party." I looked

away. "One day I just sort of put an OUT OF BUSINESS sign on my heart."

Max remained silent. Come to think of it, I couldn't remember Sam ever listening to me. Sam had always talked so much about his own life and career, he'd never really gotten to know me. "You're going to laugh, but I always had these rules I lived by. Rules that were made to keep people. . .at bay. Right now, I'm too embarrassed to even tell you what they were." I gently pulled my hand away. "But I've always avoided certain things."

"Like what?" Max studied me.

"Oh. . .you know, like women's retreats at church. I didn't want to bother with the whole bonding process. Relationships always got so messy and complicated later. I didn't do get-togethers at the clubhouse at my apartment, and I hated icebreakers of any kind." I chuckled at myself and my goofy ways, but my sudden openness felt good, so I continued. "And I disliked the greeting time at church. This is terrible, but I always arrived just after everyone had hugged." I looked at Max, wondering what he was thinking. "And I never, ever volunteered for anything. You know the housekeepers who always say they don't do windows? Well, I was the person who always said, 'I don't do people.' At least it's what my heart tried to say."

"So, how in the world did you make it in the real estate business? It's a people business."

"Dedra asked me the same thing. I guess you could say people weren't lining up to use my services."

"You hated it?" Max asked.

"At times I did. Especially when the couples wanted to tell me their entire life stories. Then they would have an argument and decide to pull their house off the market."

"Well, I think every Realtor has had a few of those."

"But then, after moving here to this house . . .to this neighborhood. . .I don't know. I see what I've missed. So many things. And I see I was living the hardest life of all. Not the way God intended. Without friends. And without. . ." My voice left me.

Max waited for me to continue, but like the sun that had just disappeared behind a cloud, I allowed the perfect moment to share more of my feelings to vanish.

"I'm so sorry, Bailey. Life has been hard on you. I won't let you get hurt again. I promise," Max said. "I do love you, and love for me is a commitment as well as a feeling."

I smiled and scooted closer to him. "It's one of the reasons I like you so much."

This time Max looked out the window. "Like?"

I tugged on the sleeve of his tux. "Please don't give up on me."

"I won't." Max touched my cheek.

Maybe I needed to lighten up. "So are you ever going to tell me where we're headed?"

"Yes. Galveston Bay."

"And are we going to hunt for shells?" I asked.

"Well, I think we're a little overdressed for the beach, but it might be fun the next time," Max said. "Actually, we're headed to Somerset Yacht Club. I own a boat jointly with my family there, so we all take turns using it. In fact, lunch is being prepared for us as we speak."

"Really? I think I could get used to this pampering thing."

—

Later that day, after we disembarked, the air engulfed us like a steam bath. I looked back at the yacht wistfully. "What a fine day. Thank you, Max."

"You're welcome." He pulled me into an embrace.

I laid my head on his shoulder as we strolled back toward the yacht club. "You know, we left so hurriedly from your grandparents' anniversary party, I didn't meet your mom and dad or your five sisters. They must think I'm rude. I am sorry about that."

"Forgiven." Max smiled. "By the way, my sisters are Evetta, Mary, Hana, Jackie, and Holly."

"Those are good names." I fiddled with my earring. "Do you think. . .they'd like me?"

"They would love you. I know there're a lot of us. We're intimidating at first, but I think they'll grow on you." Max took my hand in his as we walked. "I don't want to exaggerate. I mean, we're not the perfect family by any means. We don't agree on everything, but we all love each other, and we love the Lord. And somehow it all works."

"You make it sound so. . .charming." I squeezed his hand.

"It can be," Max said. "And my family can be a pain in the neck, too."

I laughed.

Suddenly, out of the corner of my eye, I noticed someone approaching us at a fast clip. I turned to see a man who looked familiar, but his face was covered with the brim of a baseball hat. The stranger looked up. I saw him fully, with his blue eyes and cocky manner. Oh no. What was *he* doing here? *Sam?*

19

A Demented Notion

Sam strode up to us. His eyes narrowed as he challenged us with his defiant facade. I squeezed Max's arm.

"What are you doing?" I asked Sam. "Why did you follow me here?"

"You can't walk away from me that easily," he said, slurring his words.

"Yes, I think I can. I was finished. And I think you need some new lines. Those sound like you got them from a soap opera."

Max walked up to Sam. "You're drunk. Who are you?"

Sam sneered. "None of your business."

"It is my business. I love Bailey," Max said without hesitation as he stepped up to Sam, nose to nose.

Sam stumbled but recovered. He put his hands on his hips. "Yeah, well, I loved her first. Bailey is mine."

This whole scene was more than I could endure. He was ranting like a maniac. How outrageous and childish. *Bailey, you can do this.* I stepped right up to Sam. The heavy smell of liquor made me wince in disgust. "Get ahold of yourself," I said in the most forceful voice I could muster.

Sam tottered back in shock.

"You chose to no longer be a part of my life many years ago when you married Annie." I tried to remain calm. "What made you think you could come here and claim me like some Neanderthal? It's a demented notion you'd better get rid of right now. I'm sure you made yourself sick in the head when Annie left you. I'm sorry for you."

I intensified my stare. "Your sweet mother would be so ashamed at the way you're behaving. I knew her well. I loved her. How could the son of such a wonderful woman allow himself to sink so low? I cannot help you. Only Jesus can. I would suggest you go to Him. . .no, make that *run* to Him for some real help. You've got to get over this delusion and move on with your life. Because if you follow me again, I will tell the police you're stalking me. If you go now, I won't call the police. I think it's a fair deal. I'd take it if I were you." I folded my trembling arms and stared at Sam, trying not to blink first.

Every blood vessel in Sam's face seemed to swell with rage. So much that I thought he might self-destruct. He opened his mouth and then stopped. He turned and stomped off, mumbling and cursing to himself.

As he stormed away, for a second I saw him slip something from one pocket to another. A knife. He had a knife. *Is Sam trying to send me a message?* I watched until he was out of sight. A gull let out a mournful cry somewhere. My sentiments exactly.

Max whistled softly. "Incredible. You were like this Amazon woman." He held my arms gently. "I mean, this could have turned into something really nasty, but you defused it. I'm so proud of you. I'll be telling our children this story until they tell me to be quiet."

I chuckled. Guess he didn't see Sam's knife. Maybe that's best. "It wasn't easy. I was shaking. In fact, I've never done anything like that in my life."

"Listen, I do think you got rid of the guy," Max said. "But if you ever see him come around again, I want you to tell me. Okay? There's always a chance he might want some kind of revenge."

"Okay."

"That sounds like the independent Bailey talking."

I grinned. He already knew me well. "Okay. I promise."

"Do you think he was the one who was frightening you when you first moved in?" Max looked concerned.

"I don't know." I felt a pang of guilt for not keeping Max current on all the disturbing incidents at my house, but to unload now didn't feel right either.

Max circled my waist. "Why don't we go back to the limo. I phoned Jarrett earlier. He knows we've returned."

We walked in silence for a moment. "I can't get over this," Max finally said. "So, that's the Sam you were talking about earlier." He shook his head. "I just have to know this. . . . How could you have ever fallen for him? He's nuts."

"He wasn't crazy. . .a long time ago. But life does that to people sometimes—makes deviled eggs out of them."

"Yes. Sometimes," Max said. "But. . ."

"But what?" He moved his arm up around my shoulder as we headed to the club.

"But other times"—Max grew a silly grin—"other times, Bailey, dear, life wraps you in a soft tortilla blanket and dips you in a pot of spicy salsa."

I grinned up at him. "Okay. Next outing you'll have to take me to your favorite Mexican restaurant." Life with Max just seemed so effortless and natural—as if things were happening too easily. *Bailey, don't go there.*

"It's a deal," Max said.

We strolled through the yacht club and out to the porte-cochere where Jarrett waited for us by the limo. Without warning, Max pulled me into his arms and kissed me again. Boy, I think I could get used to this. It didn't seem to matter to him in the least that people passed by grinning at us. Maybe I didn't care either.

Jarrett cleared his throat at us, and we both laughed.

"I think you've both had a good day." Jarrett winked at us as he helped us into the limo.

On the ride home, Max cradled me in his strong arms. I drifted. And drifted. And drifted until I was so sleepy I knew I'd never be able to make it all the way home awake. "Max?"

"Hmm?"

"We'd make quite a team." *Did I say that? Must have been dreaming?* The cool air and Max's woodsy scent swirled around me as I floated away on that last thought.

Sometime later, Max kissed me awake. I looked around, rubbing my eyes like a small child. I knew I must have looked silly, but he didn't laugh. He offered his hand, and I stepped out of the limo and onto the sidewalk. The afternoon sun had nearly gone home for the evening, so only the last rays lingered to play. Home again. What a day!

After Max said his sweet good-byes, I glanced across the street. I could see Magnolia hauling a wheelbarrow around the side of her house toward her backyard. To my horror I saw two cats trotting right behind her. Must be strays. Oh, no. This could be bad. Did Magnolia have an irrational fear of cats, or did she simply loathe them? Just in case her apprehension was a full-blown phobia, I decided to take things in hand and help out a neighbor in need.

I strode across the street, nearly breaking out into a run as well as a sweat. I thought of hollering to Magnolia but stopped myself for some unknown reason. I slowed my wild pace, since my heels weren't conducive to sprinting on concrete.

Magnolia disappeared through her gate with the two cats still in tow. Apparently, she had no idea what scampered just behind her. As I reached the path down the side of her house, I noticed broken pieces of some weeds sprinkled on the grass, which made a trail to the backyard. I picked up some of the plant, crushed it, and sniffed. Smelled citrus-like and, on closer inspection, looked a bit like mint with its green-gray leaves. *What is that? Oh, yeah. Catnip.* Granny had always kept some of the aromatic plant around for her cats.

But why in the world would Magnolia keep an herb in her yard that would attract the very animal she detested? If she was luring cats into her backyard, what was she doing with them? The plant fell out of my hand. A strange kind of dread welled up inside me. No. Surely not. Curiosity overwhelmed me, so I decided to allow myself just one small peek. I tiptoed, which was unnecessary since there was grass below my feet, but I was in a tiptoeing kind of mood.

The low growl of a cat filled the air—the kind of sound when you know you've got one fuming cat on your hands. What was happening? I crept up to the edge of her house and peered around the corner. In that second, Magnolia came around the bend and almost ran into me. Before I could get my bearings, I let out a shriek.

Magnolia dropped the shovel she'd been holding and let out a whoop. "Honey child. What are you doing back here?" She slapped her hand over her heart. "You scared the woolies out of me."

I suddenly felt like the criminal I was. "Well, I. . . you know. I saw cats, and so I was worried about you." That was truth. I was worried. Of course, I was also concerned for the animals, wondering if all the neighborhood cats were being bumped off one by one.

"Cats? Yes, I've got a couple strays back here. I cage 'em and then transport 'em."

"Transport them?" Was that a euphemistic way of saying she was helping them relocate to a kitty graveyard? Why was everybody in this whole neighborhood determined to act creepy? Where did all the normal people go? "Um. I'm curious. Where do you take the cats?"

"Oh, just here and yonder." She chuckled.

Dusk had settled in around us, making the backyard lights suddenly blink on. I startled for no reason. "Really? Here and yonder?"

"Honey, there're just too many stray cats around here. I'm just helping out the local agencies. They're plum overworked." Magnolia looked down with a glint in her eyes.

I followed her gaze to the shovel. The blade on the tool, which looked impressively sharp, gleamed in the porch light like some kind of eerie foreshadowing in a horror flick. Hmm. *That cat in the box must have been a stray.* But Magnolia didn't appear to have any real motive to scare me out of my house. In fact, she'd wanted me to tear it down!

"Been on a date with that handsome Mr. Max?" Magnolia raised her eyebrows.

"Uh-uh." So glad we'd moved on to another topic.

Magnolia folded her arms. "He sure is a catch. Mm. Mm. Mm."

"Yes, he is." I wondered what she'd say if she knew Max had already proposed. She'd probably make me march right over to his house and say yes.

Magnolia wiped her hands on her garden apron. "You been enjoying your house?"

I nodded. "It's slowly coming together."

"Yes, but I wondered if you liked living there."

"Why do you ask?" *Time to go home, Bailey.*

"Oh, no particular reason. Just curious." Magnolia winced.

"Are you okay?"

"Just a touch of arthritis." She picked up the shovel and leaned on it. "Thanks for asking, child."

I offered her a smile. "It's almost dark. I guess I'll head back. Good luck with your cat catching." Magnolia and I wrapped up our curious little meeting, and I strolled home in the semidarkness. As my thoughts coasted from the delights of the day with Max to the alarm of Sam's intrusion into it, I couldn't help but wonder about the latter. Why had he become so scary?

Were his harsh words going to turn into a vengeful madness? I hadn't a clue, but I hoped he wouldn't try to do anything rash—like make use of the knife I saw in his pocket. I reached out and let my fingers touch the oleanders as I breezed by them. Poisonous, weren't they? Yeah. Just like Sam.

My life had indeed moved on without him, but I knew in my heart I'd never forgiven him or grieved properly for my loss. I scurried up my walkway to my front porch. *Oh Lord, I want to forgive Sam and trust again. Hmm. Not a very profound prayer. Surely I can do better.* But before I could think of something weightier and more eloquent to say to God, tears had already started to stream down my cheeks. Right there on the porch, I wept over Sam's betrayal as well as the loss of my friend Annie.

And then I spilled the unshed tears for my loved ones now in heaven. I touched the wetness on my face, since the sensation was so unfamiliar to me. I grabbed a tissue from my purse and blew. I sighed, thinking what an odd place I'd chosen to shed my anguish and tears—and an odd place to forgive. But I did feel lighter, as if I had cut something loose from my spirit and it was flying free.

Hearing a crunching sound inside my gate, I turned around to look behind me. A woman hurried up the path toward me. I could see her face but not clearly. I dabbed at my eyes, thinking I must look like quite the red-eyed monster. "Hi there." I just hoped she wasn't going to try to sell me anything. "May I help you?" I slipped the wadded tissue into my evening bag.

"I just need a little of your time. That's all," the stranger said.

"Okay." The woman didn't look familiar to me, but something about her deep voice teased my memory.

When the woman reached the base of my porch, she looked up at me with eyes glistening with intensity. "So tell me, do you know who I am?"

I shook my head. "No, I don't think so. But I should know. Shouldn't I?"

"I'm your dear old friend Annie. . .from another life." She offered me a hollow chuckle.

I nearly collapsed right there on the porch. It took every ounce of my will to stay standing. *Annie?* I took a step toward her. We stared at each other for so long, I suddenly felt rude. "Annie Russell?"

She frowned. "Well, I was Annie Hunter, until the divorce."

"This is such a surprise. I'm. . ." I started to say, "shell-shocked," but held my tongue. Little did she know I had just been thinking about her. Forgiving her. Letting her go.

"Yeah, yeah, I know. It's hard to find me in here." She looked down at herself. "I've put on some pounds. That's what life will do to you. But you did all right so far, keeping that old lard off your hips."

"Thanks." I think. My hand covered my mouth as I still tried to absorb the moment. Amazing. After all these years, I finally forgive Annie for marrying my fiancé, and then she shows up at my house. What were the chances of that? Pretty much zero. Unless God was up to something. Was this some kind of test? If so, failure had to be imminent. But I should invite Annie inside. She may have driven all day. I could offer her coffee. Show some hospitality. Or maybe we'd just stare each other into the ground. But if I'd truly forgiven Annie for her betrayal, then coffee would seem right and good. *Okay, I'll do this for You, God.* I smiled. "Would you like to come in?"

Annie shook her head. "No. I was hoping you'd just sit with me for a while in my car." She motioned toward the black sedan parked in front of my house. "We could have ourselves a little visit."

"Sure. Okay."

She nodded but didn't smile.

Why had she come? I had no idea really, but from her demeanor, I doubted she was here to renew our friendship. I followed her down the path, noticing her tattered jeans and unkempt hair. Her body leaned a bit as if she were carrying another weight she hadn't mentioned. When we approached her car, I opened the passenger door and slid in.

Annie scooted in on the other side and turned on the interior light just above me. "There. Just what we need. A little light on the subject." That time she smiled.

Oh dear. I hoped our whole conversation wouldn't be in riddles. My body settled onto the seat. Waiting. The inside of the car looked neglected, and it reeked of cigarette butts mingled with body odor. Not a good combo. The only thing in her vehicle that came close to being cheerful was a toy airplane, which dangled from her rearview mirror. But the poor thing had faded paint and a wing broken off. I glanced over at Annie.

She sat there, lacing and unlacing her fingers. Her hands were calloused, her nails dirty. Certainly not the hands of a woman who was to marry someone with a bright political future. I swallowed any temptation to gloat. The moment felt cold, since two old friends usually went through the warm and welcoming routine of hugging and laughing and catching up. And then here we were—icicles. The kind with sharp edges. Maybe she'd come to Houston to apologize but couldn't think of the right words. "Well, so how have you been?"

"You're curious, aren't you?" Annie looked at me. "Why I'm here. Our lives didn't play out as you'd expected. Did they?" She chuckled.

"No, they didn't."

"You should know something." Annie raised her chin. "It was my idea to break up your little engagement with Sam. I chased him and flirted with him and tempted him until he became helpless to say no." She arched a defiant brow. "So tell me, what do you think of me now?"

Well, that confession wasn't what I'd expected. Or wanted to hear. "Why did you do it?" I chewed on my lower lip, not knowing if I wanted to hear more of the story.

"That's easy to answer. I fell in love with Sam. And not the way you did. Mine was real."

Her words made me flinch. "Even so, the way you both handled the situation was a little heartless. Wasn't it? I thought friends would at least—"

"You're still so naive, aren't you? Haven't you figured it out yet? Friends are disposable gloves. Use them and then toss them. But love is gold. Worth pursuing. And practically speaking, that gold pays the bills."

Annie's total lack of compassion made my whole body sag and my soul ache. But in reality, I knew I should thank her for what she did to me all those years ago. Back then, there'd only been the illusion of great loss. In the end, the turn of events had been a blessing, since I hadn't lost my life, my love. Not when God was meant to be my life and when Max was meant to be my love. But maybe a simple response was all she needed. "I forgive you, Annie." In spite of everything, I wanted to hug her, to let her know all could be well again.

She stiffened. "You've misunderstood me."

"How?"

"I didn't come here to ask for forgiveness." Annie

gave me a smirk. "But I will tell you my story. While I was still married to Sam, I met someone in the hotel where I worked, a real sweet talker named Camden Monroe. I tell you, that man could charm the wool right off a whole flock of sheep. He romanced me away from Sam the same way I romanced Sam away from you." She seemed to study me. "I thought you'd find that ironic. Or at least funny. Humph, guess not. Anyway, I thought Camden had a real promising future in Washington but came to find out his future would be in prison for mail fraud." She paused for a moment. "After it was all over with, I realized I'd made a terrible mistake. I still loved Sam."

"I'm sorry," was I could think to say.

"Why did I just tell you all that?" Annie narrowed her eyes. "Sam has come by your house to see you. Hasn't he?"

"Yes." I cleared my throat. "You know, he seemed pretty brokenhearted that you left him."

"Yeah, right. He was more like crazy angry that I dumped him." Annie lifted the flap on her camouflage purse and pulled out a cigarette. "Anyway, I heard Sam was heading to Houston to find you. So, here I am." She looked me over. "I was curious to see what he was coming after. Wanted to see how much better you looked than me." Annie stared out the car window as she tapped her fingernails against the glass. "You know, Sam still talked about you even after we were married.

And not just in the friendship way either. He never got over you. Never stopped loving you."

"I had no idea." I glanced at her but didn't want to stare. "That must have been painful."

"Oh well, that was just the villain in the story getting her just deserts." She cocked her head. "Wasn't it?"

"Please understand, I don't love Sam anymore. Not at all." Annie needed to know how far I'd moved on, and yet I felt uneasy telling her about Max.

"Guess you got yourself another man to love you. That's why you're wearing that fancy black dress. You've been on a date." Annie huffed. "Two men now. And I have none. Life just keeps getting better for you."

I gripped the car seat. "Look, I talked to Sam. There was no love in his eyes. He was confused and angry. Sam needs to rethink his life. Make some serious changes." And most of all, he needs to pray. Annie seemed to be in so much anguish, I reached out and touched her shoulder.

She jerked away, flinching as if I'd hit her. "Don't do that."

"Okay." I couldn't believe how far Annie had gotten away from all that was good. She'd always been my best friend—through dolls and birthday parties and playground bruises. And then through volleyball and acne and school plays. Friends forever, we promised each other as we linked hands in our own secret handshake. We'd even planned to raise our families next door to each other—be the best friends any neighborhood had ever seen. But all that was gone. When Annie arrived, she'd asked me if I knew who she was. But I could see now I didn't recognize her at all. She was nothing like the old Annie. And it tore at my heart. "I need to say something, if it's all right."

"What?"

"I can't help you get Sam back, but I can pray for you both." What I didn't say was that their remarriage right now would be as hazardous as setting gunpowder next to a box of matches. But somehow I didn't think she'd be open to any marital advice. Or me telling her of Sam's dangerous temper. But then Annie would have had more intimate knowledge about that subject anyway, since she'd been married to him.

"Don't pray for me." Annie's eyes darkened with what looked like hatred. "Praying for me means you think you're superior. Like you're the winner and I'm not."

My hand clutched my heart. "But this isn't a game."

"Of course it is." Annie pounded her fist on the steering wheel. "Whoever wins Sam's heart wins it all."

God, help her to believe me. "But I don't want Sam's heart."

"So you say."

I sighed, wondering how people could get things so mixed up in their heads.

Annie mumbled something. And then all the car door locks thumped down, closing us in.

Great. Now why would she do that? Perhaps Annie had become as unbalanced as Sam. I glanced down at the buttons by my elbow, but it was hard to tell for sure which one would open my door. Could I be in any danger? While Annie stared out the window watching a stray cat, I scanned the car for any object that she might decide to use as a weapon. The idea seemed ridiculous, and yet her flashes of anger frightened me. I saw a cigarette lighter on the dashboard, but I doubted she could stab me to death with such a friendly edged object. And a lighter wouldn't be the fastest way to set a moving target on fire. Unless, of course, that target was unconscious.

A chill seeped through me as the night closed in around us.

20

A Passage of Horrors

So tell me, how did you come to own this incredible house?" Annie turned back to me, smiling, her voice and attitude now as amiable as it had been in our youth. "It looks like a castle."

Seeing the old Annie startled me so much I gasped. Fortunately, she didn't seem to notice my reaction. How could her personality change so dramatically? I'd better keep talking like nothing's wrong. "Yes, Granny always wanted me to have this house. And so when she died, she left it to me." Hmm. Shouldn't have used the word "died." Once again, I studied the buttons on the side panel, trying to figure out which one to push.

"And now you're going to fix it up. . .make it into a home."

I nodded, wondering where Annie was going with the conversation. Somehow this new chat sounded even more surreal. If that were possible. "Yes, I have some pretty good plans." Someone's dog barked, and I suddenly wished I lived on a noisy bustling street. I wished Max would come whisk me away for coffee. I wished my visitor had really been a saleswoman.

"Well, please tell me more."

A drop of perspiration fell on my hand. I was sweating. Heavily. "It's kind of warm in here." I chuckled. Then I noticed a flicker of something in her expression. She could probably smell the fear on me. Not good.

Annie handed me a tissue from her purse.

I dabbed at the wetness on my face while my mouth went dry.

"You were saying?"

"Well, what exactly do you want to know about my house?"

"Oh, I don't know, Bailey. I'd like to know anything you want to tell me. I've never had a real home, except for a series of rundown apartments, so it'd be nice to hear about yours."

Okay, time to go. "It's all pretty boring stuff." I yawned. "You know what? I'm kind of tired. So if it's all right with you, I'm going to call it a night."

"But we were just starting to understand each other. Weren't we?" Annie's fingers tightened, crushing the cigarette in her hand.

"I'm not sure, really, what's happening here. To be honest, I think you have some issues you need to deal with. I wish you and Sam the very best." I pushed one of the buttons on the door, hoping it was the right one. It was. "Good night."

"But I'm being kind to you!"

I reached for the door handle and then turned back

to her. "If you think this is kindness, then you need a good book on etiquette." My voice got a little higher than I expected. "I've done you no harm, Annie. You know that."

She leaned closer to me. "You do me harm simply by being alive." Her words came out in a hiss. She reached into her purse and paused.

I should just get out of the car now. Open the door. Walk away. But for some inane reason, I felt compelled to ask more questions. "So you're hiding a gun in your purse? You actually want to shoot me? What do you think that would solve? Sam can't hold you while you're in a women's correctional facility." Why had I said that? I could have picked any words but those. I opened the car door, ready to run.

Annie pulled her hand out of her purse. "There's no gun, you fool. I had a toothpick. To dig all those fattening donut crumbs out of my teeth." Then she howled with laughter.

I was not amused. At all. It was easy to see why Annie had soured me on friendships for years.

"Oh, come on. Where's your sense of humor?" She waved me back inside. "Close the door. I want to talk about this forgiveness thing you're so obsessed about." She stuck the toothpick in her mouth and chewed.

I left the door open. It took a few seconds to calm my breathing from her dark prank. I was fairly certain Annie had no intention of discussing forgiveness, but

I stayed to give her one last chance. For what, I no longer knew.

"It's hard to forgive." The lines in Annie's face softened. "Impossible, really. But the problem is, the offenses keep piling up, and you don't know what to do with them. It gets kinda crowded in my head, shuffling and keeping tabs on them all."

"I didn't forgive you on my own. I had help."

She pressed her palms together. "Oh, I know where this one is going. The Lord will help me forgive all my debtors. Right?" Her body twitched as she turned to me. "But I choose not to forgive. How about that, Bailey Marie Walker?" She sort of sing-songed the last part.

"Well, there's always free will." I looked away. My patience was hanging by a strip of dental floss. Extra thin and waxed. Annie was just setting the table for another joke. With me as the centerpiece. "It really is time for me to go. Good-bye, Annie." I reached out to shake her hand. "Can we at least part on friendly terms?"

"I don't think so." She waved off my handshake. "Look, if you gotta go, then go." She glared at me. "Before I unleash some of my free will on you."

I did so, happily, never looking back. *Good-bye, Annie.* I speed-walked up to my porch and then breathed again. *Lord, Annie must really be in a lot of misery to be so cruel. Please help her find her way. Amen.*

Well, my prayer certainly didn't "storm heaven" as Granny always said, but at least it was sincere.

I waited for Annie to start her engine, and then I ventured a glance back at her car. Annie circled the cul-de-sac, paused, and then drove away. Her sedan rounded the corner and was soon out of sight. Gone. Just like that. At last, I let my guts unwind.

Wow. That was so random and bizarre. Not to mention ferociously unfair. It was like being sucked into an emotional time machine. Or a passage of horrors—one much worse than the one in my bedroom closet. And while I sat there sweating in Annie's car, time felt like it had crept by unnaturally. Like the earth was on beta blockers.

Groaning, I rested my head against the front door. *Honestly, Lord, why did You want to bring Annie back in my life? Seeing Sam again was bad enough. Was it just to let me see how screwed up people can get when they're in love? Not a good lesson for me right now. And if You wanted me to help her, counsel her, or witness to her, I totally blew it. I'm sorry. She caught me by surprise.*

For a moment, as I stood immovable, a question suddenly hit me—had Annie been the one—the one right from the beginning, who'd been the source of my terror? Perhaps she couldn't stand for me to have one more good thing in my life. She wanted me out of my home. Out on the street. It seemed like a real and scary possibility. But what could I do about it? Certainly nothing right this minute.

Look at it this way, Bailey; this night can't possibly get any worse. How true. And to celebrate that thought, I could take a warm shower, snuggle into bed, and read for a little while. Ahh. Good plan.

When I finally put my key in the lock, I noticed the inside of the house looked extra dark. I'd left the kitchen lights on, yet the house looked as black as the night I'd arrived. Like a dungeon. The porch light remained on, as well as the lights the landscapers had installed, but something felt wrong. Great. What now?

The perspiration on my skin turned icy as I unlocked the door and let it swing open. I've got to get that creak fixed. I flipped the switch. Funny. No lights.

What could have happened? I heard the usual buzzing sound to let me know the alarm was on, so I only had a few seconds to decide what to do. Should I risk running through the dark to turn off the alarm? I hated to make the police come roaring up for nothing and scare the whole neighborhood. *Think, Bailey.* My trusty flashlight was still by the door, so I grabbed it and sprayed the entry with light. Then I raced in to turn off the alarm.

21

Bloodcurdling Thoughts

My hand shook as I punched in the code. Was someone waiting for me in the dark? It certainly couldn't be Annie. She was long gone. Wasn't she? I made a mistake entering my code number and pushed the CLEAR button. *Come on, get it right.* I said the numbers out loud as I tapped them in again. *Okay. Alarm's off.* I let out a breath of air.

I crept through the front rooms with my flashlight, taking in every detail as I walked along. No one hid in the darkness. At least not in the front rooms. But even thug types couldn't get in with the heavy locks and alarms. Or could they? Maybe someone had just messed with my breaker box while I was gone.

I shook off the dread by singing an Irish tune my mother had loved. "Like the blooming heather on the hills. Your sweet love. . .la-la. . .I can't remember the words. . .something fills." I kept humming as I moved to the mantle area where the butterfly had been. It was as if my song was falling into a deep fissure never to be retrieved. Was there no longer an echo? Was someone standing near me to absorb the sound? A tremor exploded through me, and I whirled around in a circle with the flashlight. *Okay, Bailey, enough bloodcurdling thoughts.*

I shined the light around the fireplace. Suddenly I saw something on the wallpaper I hadn't seen before. An odd w shape. The same strange letter that had been etched on my kitchen window. I rubbed my eyes and blinked. Did that shape on the wallpaper just move? I walked closer to the black line on the wallpaper. The contours did indeed shift. Not in one jolt, but the whole of it undulated as if alive. I crept nearer, even though I really wanted to run to Max's house for safety.

This time I got close enough to decipher what was happening. Ants. Thousands of fire ants had established themselves on my wallpaper. Instead of writhing and foaming in masses like I'd seen outside on their mounds, they marched in perfects trails, forming a weird-looking *w*. But why? Were they eating the wallpaper? The glue?

I backed up for a wider view. How could mere ants make such an organized design? *Impossible. I must really be losing it big-time.*

All at once the entry lights flickered back on. Thinking someone was right behind me, I let a little shriek escape my mouth. No one stood in the entry. Relieved, I flipped on more lights.

I decided to take things in hand, literally. I got my stepladder out of the hall closet, and even though I was still adorned in my black spaghetti-strapped dress, I began scooping up the ants with wads of damp toilet paper. One of the pests bit me, and I flicked him across the room.

As I scraped along, I noticed a faint line left even after the ants were gone. Someone had smeared something on the wallpaper. I picked off a piece of the material and sniffed it. I really didn't know, but it appeared to be honey. But why would someone smear something on my wallpaper for the ants to eat? And how did the ants find it? At least the stuff, whatever it was, didn't seem fresh. No one had been in the house recently; otherwise it would still be gooey.

Annie came to mind again, and I wondered how far she might go to hurt me. Hard to know for sure. On one hand, she may have only wanted to check me out, throw around a little intimidation, and then make certain I wasn't going to interfere with her plans to win Sam back. On the other hand, she could already be a dangerous problem. But whoever it was, I didn't want to receive anymore ant bouquets!

In a fit of indignation, I dumped the bundles of ants into a bucket. I plugged up the tiny crawl hole on the baseboard with a squirt from my caulking gun and then flushed the wads of paper and insects down the commode. I'd come to know fire ants intimately since living in the Bayou City. I'd been bitten ferociously too many times to count, and I was in no mood to show compassion toward them. In fact, I wished miserable things on their wretched little lives.

Back to reality. So, was the design on the wallpaper some sort of message like the one on the kitchen window? Or maybe it was just to make me crazy. Like a frog allowing itself to get cooked to death one degree at a time, I wondered if the ploy was slowly working on me and I just didn't know it yet.

I suddenly realized that someone must have flipped the lights back on in my breaker box. Why hadn't I thought of that before? I ran to kitchen door and turned on the porch lights. I craned my neck to see out in the darkness. The landscaping lights illuminated part of the backyard, but there were so many pockets of blackness, anyone could be hiding. Should I open the door and check it out, or should I call Max? Why did I need to bother him when I could do the same thing? *Safety in numbers, and he's stronger.*

Ignoring my own warnings, I stepped out into the backyard. With my flashlight in hand, I sneaked over to the breaker box. I saw what I needed to see. The door to the box was indeed open, yet I remembered the electrician closing it the day before.

I scanned the yard in a frantic search but saw no one running, trying to escape. No movement at all, except for the rhythmic swaying of the Spanish moss hanging like silver hair on the live oaks. I could hear the comments of the tree frogs and crickets. The sounds seemed tranquil in contrast to my strange and anxious night queries.

After giving up on the intruder, I decided, at least, to check out one more lead. I was curious what could have coaxed the ants into my house over the fireplace. With a purposeful gait, I headed to the west side of the house. Once I saw the extension where the flue would be, I flashed the light around the base of the house. I noticed a blob of something. I leaned in to see the alien sight more clearly. Goo of some kind had been smeared over a weep hole.

I touched the slimy substance and then took a whiff. "It's sticky and smells like honey," I whispered to no one. *So, that's how the ants got started.* Then I had another revelation. Maybe someone had primed the area over the mantle with the honey before I put in the doors and security. Then he or she recently added the honey outside to encourage the ants inside. *Okay, that's pretty farfetched, Bailey.* But I didn't want to believe people still had access to the inside of my home.

I turned on the water hose and sprayed the honey away from the weep hole. I reminded myself to put down a load of ant poison in the morning. I turned off the water and glanced around again. All looked clear.

As I headed to the back door, my brain was racked with questions again. What did the repeated *w* pattern mean? It didn't look like a real *w*, yet it seemed familiar to me. I kept thinking of students and class. The filing cabinets of information in my brain suddenly uncovered something. . .a morsel of potentially vital information. The *w* wasn't really a *w*. It was meant to symbolize something else.

During high school, one of the teachers had tried to pound some Greek into all his students. Including me. I remembered only bits, but it was easy to recall the symbols for the alpha and the omega. The uppercase Greek letter for omega was well known, but the smaller case letter stayed in my head because it looked like the top of a pitchfork. The odd looking letter also represented "omega." And, of course, omega meant. . .the end.

I shivered even though the temperature was almost eighty. Feeling spooked, I slipped through the open door and secured it. I felt as though someone's strange amusements, which had all been at my expense, were now taking a more sinister turn.

All right. Calm yourself and think. As I paced through the house, I remembered a miniscule but significant fact from high school—Annie and Sam had never taken Greek. Whoever was putting on these dark theatrics wanted to show me how smart and clever he or she was. And neither Sam nor Annie had ever been academically inclined or particularly clever. I squelched what would have been a satisfying grin.

I officially checked Sam and Annie off as culprits, but now I'd have to go back, looking at the others in question. I suppose eventually, though, everyone looked guilty. In fact, if I concentrated hard enough, I could probably incriminate myself!

Then a thumping noise in the library stopped my reverie as well as my heart. "Who's there?" Had someone gotten in while I'd been outside? I stood motionless, except for the tremor in my legs. There was the noise again. Someone was in the house. Or was it the usual creaks and moans from the ancient timbers?

I wanted to move, but I couldn't budge. I bit my lip and propelled myself toward the library. "Who's there?" *Why did I keep saying that?*

As I stood just outside of the library, I held my breath and reached my hand into the dark room. Was someone just around the corner? I flipped the switch on quickly and peered inside. No one. Light now filled every corner of the library. Nothing. How odd. "What's happening here?" Just existing in this house of shadows and echoes was becoming agonizing. It was hard to know what was real and what was created merely from the momentum of my own imaginings.

I noticed a moth battering himself against the bare bulb, his wings crumbling against the heat. He had no idea freedom was all around him. I shooed him away from the light, not wanting anything else to be tortured.

I checked the whole house again for unwanted visitors and then headed into my bedroom for some sanctuary. As I sat down on my bed, I heard a scratching noise. What now? The two-way radio had come to life again. I'd kept fresh batteries in it, and now my diligence had paid off.

This time I heard a man with a heavy accent. He yelled, "Where have you been? Answer me!" Then the man mumbled, or perhaps he'd pulled the device away from his mouth so he could talk to someone near him. I positioned the radio tightly against my ear, straining to hear every sound. *Eva.* Yes, he definitely had said the name *Eva.* He was talking to her, muttering about *Volstead.* I heard him say a few words I couldn't make out, but after a few seconds of interference, I heard him murmur something to Eva that included the word *Lakes.*

As I absorbed those last words, the radio slipped from my hand and fell onto the wooden floor. I looked down at the gadget. The green light had gone out even though the batteries were new. I had broken the two-way radio.

THIS DARK JOURNEY

Mr. Lakes. Well, he'd certainly acted oddly the day he'd handed me the deed and key, and he'd mentioned something about the house having an unwholesome feeling. Lakes couldn't have been more right. I just had no idea some of the unwholesomeness might be him.

And Eva—the wife of Boris Lukin. The two of them were my next-door neighbors. The ones always hiding behind the trees and shrubs. I suddenly remembered something Max had said—that the Lukins had wanted to buy Volstead Manor.

I slid down to the floor. Okay. What do I have so far? The first time the radio had been in use, I had overheard the voice of an angry woman. That may have been Eva Lukin, although I couldn't remember for certain if the woman had an accent. Eva had talked to someone named Seth about a plan not working. Now a man with a thick accent talked about my house, and then he mentioned the name *Lakes* as he spoke to Eva. What was the man's accent? Romanian? Magnolia had said the Lukins came from a village in Transylvania. That fact was certainly easy to remember. Yes, indeed, the data leads to the Lukins' house. It would also explain how I could hear the two-way radio, since the house wasn't far away.

Other intriguing particulars kept seeping into my thinking. I felt certain Granny's attorney, Mr. Lakes, was mixed up in the plan since his name was mentioned. That means Lakes must have been the one to alert the Lukins of my arrival. Made sense. I picked up the two-way radio. Also, a person named Seth, who appeared to be the owner of the gadget, was somehow involved. And apparently Boris and Eva were livid, wondering why Seth hadn't stayed in touch.

I gripped the radio in my palm until it made my hand ache. I released it and noticed what I had not noticed before. The black device had wear marks on it from heavy use. Some of the shiny paint had worn off where Seth's fingers had been. They were marks from much smaller hands than mine. The hands of a child. Seth was not an adult.

Then I recalled the small ghostlike figure who had run through my backyard one evening. Perhaps that figure had been Seth. There had also been the strange flashing light, like Morse code, coming from the Lukins' upstairs window, which I'd not only seen that same evening, but also on the night I'd moved in. And what about the Morse code I'd seen? Had I really caught the Lukins spelling out the word *cat*?"

I rubbed my temples to help my concentration. I couldn't help but wonder if other people were involved.

And more important, what exactly was the plan Eva mentioned to Seth? My house wasn't worth much, and Granny's money had been a secret. I'd been down that rabbit hole before, and it only went in circles.

I sighed and focused on something else Max had said. He'd mentioned a man named Buford who had desperately wanted the house and who'd been willing to pay much more than it was worth. Max had also said the offer had come in years earlier. That was long before Granny had even placed the money in the passageway. So, there must be something else enticing about my house.

Oh Lord, please help me figure out the "whys" of this. You and I are still in this together. Right?

The terms *Prohibition* and *Volstead* suddenly rang in my head for attention. There was the still in the attic as well as the strange passage in my bedroom closet, which did appear to be designed as part of the house when it was built. The long, narrow hole with the ladder was obviously a hidden storage for the alcohol, which the homeowners were trafficking illegally.

But surely no one would be interested in a few jars of alcohol, especially since some of the booze made back during Prohibition had turned out to be poisonous. I doubted the canning jars were worth a great deal, but maybe there was something else hidden in the house—money, jewels, or valuables of some kind that were interconnected with the business of bootlegging.

For some reason, a poem from a recent mystery, *Too Close to the Flame*, surfaced in my mind. A couple of the lines went something like:

"Shall I come to fasten or tear apart,
to love or veil this blueprint on my heart?"

"Blueprint," I whispered. Interesting word, which brought something else to mind—something I'd seen in the attic. When I'd looked into the compartment where the still was hidden, I had also seen a wrinkled piece of paper, bluish in color, like a blueprint. I wondered if the paper could be a true layout of the house. If the document was real, could it show any other secret passages? And might those hidden spaces contain something rare and valuable? Unfortunately, though, the blue paper had appeared unreachable that day. *Maybe I can remove a few of the attic boards.*

I glanced down at my clothes. I still had on my heels and black dress. The outfit wasn't a good fit for the evening's agenda, but I didn't want to waste any more time.

With flashlight in hand, I bounded up both flights of stairs to the third floor. As I reached for the attic doorknob, I felt a ripple of regret for not telling Max all about the recent events. He did know about Granny's money as well as some of the original unpleasant incidents, but all the current happenings hadn't been mentioned to him. Or to anyone.

If Max could see me now, he'd think I was leading a double life. One minute I was the quirky Bailey who he hoped had potential as a wife and friend, and then there was that other side—the Bailey who couldn't commit to anyone or trust anyone or even call the police when she was pursued by scoundrels!

I needed Max's help. I wanted his help. And yet I was a woman on a mission, and to stop now and explain all the facts would most certainly slow everything down. Not to mention that Max would insist I call the police. I would refuse, and then we'd be at an impasse. Well, I'd started on this dark journey, and I was determined to finish it.

I opened the door to the attic, turned on the light, and climbed up on the stack of wood near the far corner. I shined my flashlight down the opening. With only a little strain, I saw the bluish document again but couldn't reach it. Hmm. If I managed to rip off one of the boards at the bottom, I might be able to reach in and slip the paper out. I proceeded to rip off a loose board with the heel of my shoe. *Well, at least I'll get some good out of these silly things.*

I then wallowed on the dirty floor in my dress, trying to stretch my hand into the narrow opening. I felt for the paper, found it, and gingerly eased it out. A task that should have been impossible, or at least tricky, became almost too easy.

The paper did appear to be a blueprint of some kind. I placed the document on a nearby crate and smoothed out the wrinkles. I moved my finger along the faded lines, trying to find something familiar. After a few seconds of probing, I found the living room, kitchen, library, as well as the other rooms. Then I saw the second floor bedrooms and even the tower on the third floor. The document did indeed appear to be the original blueprint of the house.

I quickly zeroed in on my bedroom closet. Would the hidden space be indicated? Yes, there were extra parallel lines—a passage had been designed into the walls between the two bedroom closets. *My goodness.* Guess the owners had to bribe the architect as well as the builder to keep quiet. Or maybe the owners just claimed they wanted a place to keep their valuables, and then they simply added their own shelving later.

A drop of sweat fell from my forehead and splattered on the document. I dabbed up the wetness with the hem of my dress. I noticed not far from the damp spot was a circle with an *x* inside, which had been drawn in separately within the passage. *Looks like someone has drawn the lines in with black ink.*

I had this gut feeling I was about to discover something. If I could understand the motives of my tormentors, I might think of a way to outsmart them.

I felt invigorated yet unexpectedly spooked as if someone were watching me. I looked over my shoulder.

No one was there. *Calm down, Bailey.*

Without delay, I folded up the blueprint and headed downstairs to my bedroom closet. I stared at the false door, which I hadn't opened since my first morning in the house. The ladder had looked so precarious, I hadn't wanted to risk my life for exploration's sake. Now I needed to know. I had to get some answers. Right now.

I remembered the procedure. I lifted the section of the wainscotings that had been made as a separate unit and slid the door all the way up until it locked into place. I positioned my flashlight to shine into the hole. Oh, if those walls down there could talk, the stories they might tell. *Enough postulation. Let's see.* Okay, my shoes weren't going to work. I yanked off my heels and got on my knees. I backed into the hole before I could talk myself out of going. I eased my foot down ever so slowly to find the first rung of the ladder.

Odd smells tickled my nostrils as my foot settled down on the first board. The wood felt solid enough. Okay. Next rung and then the next. Nothing felt wobbly, so I hung on with one hand and reached up for the flashlight with the other. Leaning back, I set the light behind me on a shelf between two jars of home brew. Now I could see what I was doing.

The map had shown the mark to be just right of the door, but how far down, I had no idea. With great care, I lowered myself farther down into the passage.

The air chilled my overheated skin, making me feel feverish. I glanced downward into the black pit. My hands went weak, thinking of the consequences of a fall. *Bailey Marie Walker, whatever you do, don't look down!*

I froze in place to calm my thoughts. *Breathe in. Breathe out.* Okay. I searched the inner wall for signs of anything that might look like a secondary entry. Hmm. If I were trying to hide something, how would I do it? Possibly with yet another sliding door? But wouldn't that be too obvious? Just as I flirted with that thought, I moved a couple of jars of spirits and noticed an area between the shelves that looked slightly different. As I held on, I let my other hand feel the surface of the wood. The tips of my fingers felt a slight notch in one of the boards.

I looped my arm under the rung of the ladder for a little extra support and safety, and then with my other hand, I tried to grip the notch and pull. Something shook loose. I swung a bit to the right for some leverage. I tried again, and bit by bit the miniature door slid to the left. A hole. I couldn't believe it. A small hidden space had been exposed.

I leaned closer to the opening. The flashlight did little to illuminate the hole. Did I really want to stick my hand in there? I gritted my teeth and plunged my fist inside. I spread my fingers as something wispy lighted on my hand. Oh, great. Spiderwebs. Those creatures certainly weren't my best friends. Maybe they were all asleep. Just keep going.

Then my hand hit something hard. I felt around the object. It was a box with handles! Wow. I wanted to cheer. I wanted to find Max and kiss him. But not yet. I had more work to do.

In one sweep, I pulled the box out of the hole. Dust stirred and hovered around my head, making me cough and sneeze.

I could see the box was really a small antique looking chest. I couldn't believe it. A rush of satisfaction and relief washed over me. Even if the box turned out to be empty, I didn't care. I'd found it. Yes indeed. I'd finally discovered the engine that had driven a small cluster of folks over the edge.

No time for reflection, Bailey. My arms were starting to ache, so I pushed my hand through one of the circular handles and started up the ladder. The box wasn't weighty, but the metal still cut into my wrist. With speed that surprised even me, I hauled the chest up, hollering all the way up for oomph. I heaved the box up onto the ledge. Next, I retrieved the flashlight and sat it next to the box. Now, to get me out of here.

I reached up to grab the edge of the closet, but my sweaty hands lost their grip. I slipped downward, screaming. My arms thrashed about, trying to find something to grasp. I heard a ripping sound and then felt a slight jolt. Stunned, but grateful, I saw that the flared part of my dress had caught on a sharp piece of protruding wood. With only my leg caught in a rung of the ladder and my dress precariously holding me, I semi dangled in terror for a moment. With adrenaline-laced strength, I grabbed a wooden shelf and then the ladder. *Got it. Thank you, Lord.*

Once attached again, I gave the ladder the clutch of death. I felt funny hugging two-by-fours like that, but I couldn't help myself. After a consoling pause, I reached out ever so carefully and released my dress from the spike of wood. Then I hoisted myself back up into the light. Freedom at last.

I rested back on my closet floor, horizontal and motionless. My teeth felt gritty. I licked my lips and swallowed. I stayed there without moving until the horror of what had nearly happened faded a bit.

I suddenly realized why someone would want to create another separate compartment in the passage. If anyone unsympathetic to their business were to find the goods, at least the cash would still be safe. Safe to launder or use for bribes or hold until the Volstead Act could be repealed. I raised an eyebrow. Sounded logical. And since there were so many remaining jars, the owners must have been forced to leave in a hurry. Could they have been murdered by the mob? If so, the house may have been abandoned, controlled by the state, and then auctioned off.

Hmm. Even though Granny never lived in the

house and it had fallen into disrepair, I wondered if she'd been the one to modernize it since the '20s. I shook my head. Only God knew the answers to all my queries.

I switched gears and thought of Max again. I wondered what he would have thought if he could have seen me carry that chest up from the depths of the house. Would he be proud of me or would he be upset that I didn't call the police? Maybe a little of both. I chuckled.

Still resting on my back, I lifted my hand to assess the cut on my wrist. A pearl of blood seemed suspended in the air and then plunged onto my forehead. I dabbed at the blood with the hem of my dress.

I rose to my feet and looked at myself, appraising my evening dress. The goofy thing was hopelessly tattered and filthy. Oh well. Even though the dress hadn't really done that much for my figure, it had helped save my life. I was one grateful woman.

I finally turned my attention to the chest. There it sat, sort of glaring at me. Grimy. Tarnished. And probably empty. How apropos. I almost wanted to forget about the box now, since it had been the source of all my troubles.

But after a few more seconds, I succumbed to my inquisitive nature and situated myself on the bed with the chest on my lap. The latch looked corroded. What did I expect? I pulled on the fastener and lifted the lid, which made the hinges moan in protest.

Inside were permanent dividers for cash, but the only objects in the box were miscellaneous belongings: a watch, an empty perfume bottle, a photograph of a woman, a faded red hanky with embroidered edges, a tarnished key, and two stray green marbles. The twin glass balls seemed to look up at me like the eyes from the dead cat I'd found on the night of my arrival. I shivered, remembering that poor lifeless animal, now buried in my backyard. I picked up the key and held it up to the light. *Hmm. I wonder what this might open. Probably just an old door key.* I tossed it back inside. After removing the photo from the chest, I quickly closed the lid.

I shook my head and sighed. There inside were the answers to so many of my questions—the finale to the greedy quest. No money. No treasure. No valuables of any kind. Just a rusty brass chest with a few mementoes. "Don't store up treasures on earth," I said aloud.

As I ran my finger across the yellowed photograph, I wondered who the woman was. Could she still be alive? Did she actually sell the liquor that lined the walls of the passage? With her Victorian hair and dress, the woman certainly didn't look like a bootlegger. I placed the photograph on my night table next to my beta fish, Liberty.

I sighed and shook my head. The past few weeks were too staggeringly clear. Mr. Lakes, Boris and Eva Lukin, Seth, and perhaps others, had conspired to find the chest in the passage in my closet. Yet the box was mostly empty. No cash or treasure. They had won nothing. I had lost my peace of mind. It was definitely a lose-lose situation.

What could I do? I desperately needed closure. Now.

I recalled the final plot twist in my favorite mystery, *Another Stab at Life,* which was a bizarre cat-and-mouse story. The central character, a Realtor named Whittaker, searches for his sister who had turned up missing. After deciphering a series of clues, he is grief stricken to find his sister in an abandoned house, stabbed to death. Since they had both witnessed a recent burglary, he knows the thief will stop at nothing to kill him as well. Whittaker is soon pursued by the killer in what becomes a mysterious and deadly game. He becomes weary of being chased and desperate to see justice served for the crime against his sister, so he suddenly decides to face his foe head on. No more flight. Whittaker ends the journey—forcing a collision with the truth.

Hmm. I like that. Of course, that method had nearly gotten the hero killed, but I still felt the technique had some merit. So why couldn't I just give Boris and Eva a little call? Oh yeah. We could have a neighborly chat. I didn't have the phone number, but after a trot downstairs and a call to information, I had their home number. But would the Lukins even pick up their phone since Magnolia said they never answered their door? Would they have Caller ID? Somehow I doubted it, since they used such primitive tools as Morse code and walkie-talkies.

I scribbled some notes on a notepad to help me with my peculiar little speech. I sent up a prayer for courage and picked up the phone. One ring. Two rings. Maybe I should hang up. Three rings. Someone picked up the phone, yet no one said "hello." I could hear the faintest breathing. Either Boris or Eva was listening.

Okay, here goes. "Hi. This is Bailey Walker, your new next-door neighbor. The reason for my call is. . .I wanted you to know I'm not afraid anymore, and I'm not leaving. The chest was found, and it contains no money and no treasure." I paused to catch my breath. No response came except ragged breathing.

A woman cleared her throat on the other end of the line. Then I heard some faint arguing. She must have covered the speaker with her hand so she could hash it out with Boris.

"We've no idea what you're talking about," the woman said in a heavy accent. "But. . .we were planning. . .to sell our house anyway. In fact, we were on our way outside to put up a FOR SALE sign when you interrupted us."

I couldn't help but notice her haughty air sputtering and dissolving into panic. "Well, all right then." I wasn't sure what to say next. Eva's statement had taken me by surprise. "Good night." My hand shook so violently, I couldn't get the phone back on the cradle. I steadied myself and sighed. *Okay, you done good.*

I leaned against the kitchen counter and let out a long breath. I just hoped the Lukins were indeed the perpetrators. If, by some wild chance, they weren't the offenders, and they really didn't know what I was talking about, then the Lukins would certainly think they had a very troubled neighbor named Bailey who needed some serious psychiatric help. But even though Eva didn't offer a confession, her voice had betrayed her.

All of a sudden I felt like crumpling to the floor in a heap. Was it over? Surely they would give up now. I decided to celebrate prematurely with some coffee. Yes, a big honking stay-awake-all-night pot of French roast. I intended to stay up just in case there was a momentous event—the unveiling of the FOR SALE sign on the front lawn of my inimitable neighbors, Boris and Eva Lukin. I laughed out loud. Hadn't done that in a while in my own home. It felt good to seize the day.

Later, as I poured myself some steaming coffee from the pot, I let my mind wander back to the dark passageway. Dangling in that shadowy space had reminded me of something. Oh yeah. Like the way my life had looked over the past couple of years. Without friends and family, or love and hope. *But I've opened my heart a little, God. Haven't I? Isn't that what you and Granny teamed up to do?*

But really, I'd experienced so much more than just a fissure in my hard, cynical heart. I'd learned to trust once more. To truly love again. I could no longer keep my feelings buried. I loved Max. I love him with my whole heart. In fact, I felt the urge to tell him now— tell the whole world right this very minute. What time was it? I didn't really care. I would fix up a little and then go over to tell him the news. But he loves me with messy hair and dirty clothes. What beautiful words. The time was now.

I slipped on my shoes, thinking of his endearing smile as he would wake up and wonder why I'd come. Just as I turned to leave, I noticed a tall figure in my backyard, illuminated by the ornamental lights. Not at all the boy, Seth, I'd seen before. Funny, it almost looked like Max. I moved closer to the kitchen window. It was indeed Max. But why? What was he doing in my backyard at this time of night? He was in bed. Wasn't he?

I wanted to rush into Max's arms, but something held me back. Instead of going to him, I watched this man I loved as he searched the ground. What was he looking for—the two-way radio? But I hadn't even told him about the walkie-talkie. Then a thought came to me that was too terrifying to believe. Had Max been involved with the Lukins' plan all along? And what about Dedra? Was she caught up in the deceit as well? Perhaps they would still believe there was a treasure, and they wouldn't give up or let anyone stop them. Had Granny somehow been in the way and had to be silenced? Had I come to this place, lonely and afraid, only to land in a nest of treachery and murder?

PLEASE CATCH ME

I steadied myself against the counter, thinking I might pass out. *No, God. Please don't let it be.* But even as I prayed, words of accusation filled my head.

I balled my fingers into a fist so tightly I winced, but the twinge of pain was nothing compared to what I felt as I stared out into the night. Another love would be lost. Another trust broken. This time, I knew, I would never recover.

Max picked up what looked like a notebook. He didn't even bother looking around to see if he was being watched. I suddenly felt ashamed, wondering if I'd jumped to conclusions. Had the multitude of mysteries I'd read somehow distorted my perception of reality? Had I given up on trust and love so easily? What was I made of anyway—paper and air? *No more, Bailey. I will take this leap of faith before I know all the answers. Even if I'm dead wrong. I'm leaping, God. Please catch me!* I unlocked the door and rushed outside toward Max.

He opened his arms. "Bailey. What's happened? Did Sam do this to you?" His voice held concern mingled with anger.

I shook my head and clung to Max. I noticed he had on PJs and no shoes. He must have left in a hurry.

"I can see a bit of your backyard from my bedroom window," Max said. "I thought I saw someone back here. I thought it might be Sam." He gently pulled me away to look into my eyes. "Why didn't you answer the phone or the door earlier? I got so worried, I almost called the police."

There was such love, such tenderness and concern in Max's voice, I knew that the emotion I'd been holding back was about to blow. The passion of my sentiments—the absolute relief—started with a single tear and then turned into a real gusher. But instead of making me feel childish, Max stroked my head and said all manner of soothing things until I could calm down. Nothing had ever felt so good. All the doubts and fears ended right there. "Thank you, Max," I whispered.

"Now will you tell me what happened to you? You've got blood on your face. And look what I found. A notebook in your backyard with the name *Seth* on it."

"Seth is a boy. And now I'm beginning to think he wants to be caught. Maybe he got tired of the game."

Max looked at me with a mixture of surprise and bewilderment.

"I have some things I need to tell you. But first, I need to look at the Lukins' front yard."

"You mean Eva and Boris?" Max asked. "Why?"

"Humor me." I touched his cheek. "I have to know

if they've put out a FOR SALE sign."

"I've always hoped they would move, but what makes you think they might?"

Max did humor me. We walked down the sidewalk and peeked around the trees and shrubbery, which separated our properties. I gasped when I saw Boris busily hammering a FOR SALE sign into their front lawn. Eva was shouting at him in her native tongue. Apparently, Boris had gotten the sign crooked. I nodded, satisfied, so we headed back inside.

"Now will you please tell me why we needed to see that?" Max looked amused and curious.

"Max, I have a lot to tell you. I just made a pot of coffee. Want some?"

"Got decaf?" Max asked.

"No."

He shrugged. "Okay."

"Now that's love." I poured Max a steaming mug of coffee and began my tale from the very beginning. "Well, it all started with a passage."

"You mean the hole you talked about. . .where your grandmother left you the money?"

"Yes, that's it. But there's a bit more there than just a hole." We both sat down, and I explained the passage in detail.

Max glanced up. "The jars still have moonshine in them?"

"Some do," I said.

Max's face flooded with surprise. "You're kidding. Right?"

"No. I'm not."

"Incredible. So, when are you going to show me this amazing closet?"

"Tonight, if you'd like. But I still have a great deal to explain." Then I told Max about the walkie-talkies, the ants on the wall over the mantle, Mr. Lakes, Seth, the Lukins, the chest, and every other detail I could think of along the way that I hadn't told him before. I even mentioned my strange encounter with Annie.

When the pot of coffee had been drained and I'd gone through my long and arduous account, Max raked his hand through his hair. "No wonder your grandmother hired me to watch out for you. She knew you needed it."

I smiled.

"Why didn't you tell me everything that was going on?"

"I wish I had now. Oh, I'm so sorry, Max. I promise I won't do that again. Will you ever forgive me?"

He huffed a bit and then sighed. "You are exasperating, Bailey Marie Walker. But you figured it all out on your own. Amazing. All of it. I'm so proud of you." Max pulled me into a hug. "But I still think we should have called the police."

I grinned again. More warmly this time. Things were going better than I'd hoped. And someday when the time was right, I'd tell Max about the suspicions and doubts I'd courted and how some of them had gotten absurdly out of control. But not right now. The time had come for something else. "Max. I love you. I should have said it before. I want to be your wife. I want you to be my husband. Love and cherish. The whole thing. Marry me, please."

Max appeared stunned. Like I'd done something he'd never expected.

"You haven't changed your mind?" I suddenly felt anxious. "Have you?" In spite of the blood, sweat, and tears, Max kissed me thoroughly. And I thoroughly enjoyed kissing him back.

Max snuggled in my hair and neck. "Maybe we could get married tomorrow."

He sat down on a chair, and I sat on his lap as if I belonged there. Which I did.

"Hey." Max hugged me to him.

"Hey, yourself." I touched his face. A little scratchy, but who was I to talk? My dress was dirty and torn, my hair had become a nest for vermin, and my makeup had melted down to my chin. Not a pretty sight.

"Well, you've been through quite a bit today," Max said. "I'll have another story to tell our kids. . .which they will never believe." He dampened a napkin and gently wiped the dirt and blood off my face.

I smiled most genuinely at Maxwell Sumner, the man who I'd marry. Out of the blue, I thought of my huge set of Fostoria dishes Granny had left me—the ones I was convinced I'd never use. With the size of Max's family, I'd have to dust them off and learn how to cook in army-sized portions. Maybe Granny had planned the whole thing right down to the dishes.

"And so when do you want to marry?" Max took my hands in his.

I wiped the September heat from my brow. "Sometime when it's not so humid. So my hair won't droop and my skin won't be covered with this. . .slimy film."

"Trust me," Max said. "You'll get used to the humidity here. After awhile it feels more like. . .a warm comforting bath."

I gave Max an imploring expression.

"Okay. I know you brides like to keep fresh, so we sometimes get our first cool front in say. . .late September."

"But that's right away. How about a wedding around Thanksgiving? I have a lot to be thankful for."

"Okay," Max said. "Sounds like a good idea."

I did indeed like the way I felt in Max's arms. Couldn't imagine ever tiring of it. "So I guess the deal Granny made with you is off. You're no longer my brother-type guy friend watching out for me?"

"Right. Now I'll be your husband-type guy friend watching out for you."

I nodded. "I think I can handle it." I reached up and touched Max's hair, moving a lock or two out of place. "You know, if Granny were here, I'd tell her you did a good job finding me a husband."

Max chuckled.

Then I reminded him I expected a delivery of my engagement ring early the next morning. I guess he liked the idea, because we celebrated our appointment with another slow kiss.

In spite of the day's rip-roaring ride, I fell into bed with the most serene and glorious emotions. I was now officially Max's one and only. Guess we'd have to carve our initials in that old oak after all.

As I snuggled into the goosey softness of my bed, I glanced over at Granny's sack of seeds on the night table. Tomorrow morning I thought I might try planting a few of those seeds. See how they'd grow.

Suddenly, a few lines of Granny's letter came to mind. Her simple declaration had rung true like a clear sounding bell, and I knew I would encourage my own children with the same words someday. *Always talk to the One who created you. Even when things seem too dark or too impossible. He's the God of redemption and of love. In fact, He's watching out for you, even now.*

I turned over and gazed at my little beta friend in the pink glow of the nightlight. He sort of boogied around in the bowl, and if he were capable of smiling back at me, I think he just might do that. "Sweet dreams, Liberty."

EPILOGUE

Boris and Eva procured a Realtor the very next day. I decided not to press charges, even though the Lukins did turn out to be the masterminds behind all the dark deeds. Boris and Eva sold their house in record time and then decided to return to their homeland, which was a village in the heart of Transylvania.

Mr. Lakes, Granny's attorney, who'd been paid by the Lukins to dispense bits of information concerning my comings and goings, disappeared suddenly and was never seen again.

Max and I found Seth Martin in my backyard the morning after our engagement. Apparently, the ten-year-old Seth had become concerned about visiting juvenile detention, so he came clean. Seth had agreed to help the Lukins frighten me into selling my home. Boris and Eva intended to buy Volstead Manor and then find and split the so-called bootleg treasure. Except for my inheritance from Granny, no fortune or jewels were discovered in the passage.

Because of my growing curiosity in knowing how the Lukins came to find out about the treasure, we questioned Seth further and discovered Eva Lukin had overheard someone speaking of it. Seth claimed Eva never saw the man she'd overheard, since she was busy hiding behind a cedar tree as the man talked on a cell phone. In our inquiry, we also learned that Seth was a distant relative of the Lukins, which may have been why Boris and Eva trusted Seth to join their scheme.

Since Seth had no previous criminal record, we offered him a pleasant choice—the risk of having charges pressed against him or the willingness to serve fifty hours of community service, which would be supervised by his mother and our neighbor, Miss Magnolia Waters. Without delay, Magnolia found Seth a position washing dishes at the homeless shelter run by the good folks at Mount Zion Gospel Church.

And me? Well, I got this one-of-a-kind house full of mysteries from my Granny Minna Short as well as a neighborhood full of eccentric but good friends.

Best of all, though, I got Max.

Award-winning author **Anita Higman** has twenty books published for adults and children and five novels coming out. She has been honored in the past as a Barnes & Noble "Author of the Month" for Houston.

Anita has a B.A. degree from SNU combining speech communication, psychology, and art. She lives with her family near Houston, Texas.

Some of Anita's favorite things are reading, going to the movies, public speaking, and cooking brunch for her friends. She'd love for you to visit her Web site at www.anitahigman.com.

You many correspond with this author by writing:
Author Relations
PO Box 721
Uhrichsville, OH 44683

A Letter to Our Readers

Dear Reader:

In order to help us satisfy your quest for more great mystery stories, we would appreciate it if you would take a few minutes to respond to the following questions. We welcome your comments and read each form and letter we receive. When completed, please return to:

Fiction Editor
Heartsong Presents—MYSTERIES!
PO Box 721
Uhrichsville, Ohio 44683

Did you enjoy reading *Another Stab at Life* by Anita Higman?

Very much! I would like to see more books like this!
The one thing I particularly enjoyed about this story was:

_____
_____
_____

Moderately. I would have enjoyed it more if:

_____
_____
_____

Are you a member of the HP—MYSTERIES! Book Club?
Yes   No

If no, where did you purchase this book?

_____

Please rate the following elements using a scale of 1 (poor) to 10 (superior):

___ Main character/sleuth   ___ Romance elements

___ Inspirational theme   ___ Secondary characters

___ Setting   ___ Mystery plot

How would you rate the cover design on a scale of 1 (poor) to 5 (superior)? _____

What themes/settings would you like to see in future **Heartsong Presents—MYSTERIES!** selections? _____
_____
_____
_____

Please check your age range:
- ○ Under 18   ○ 18–24
- ○ 25–34   ○ 35–45
- ○ 46–55   ○ Over 55

Name: _____

Occupation: _____

Address: _____

E-mail address: _____